CHUCK DIXON
WINTERWORLD
THE MECHANIC'S SONG

Become our fan on Facebook **facebook.com/idwpublishing**
Follow us on Twitter **@idwpublishing**
Check us out on YouTube **youtube.com/idwpublishing**
Instagram **youtube.com/idwpublishing**
deviantART **idwpublishing.deviantart.com**
Pinterest **pinterest.com/idwpublishing/idw-staff-faves**

978-1631402357   18 17 16 15   1 2 3 4

Ted Adams, CEO & Publisher
Greg Goldstein, President & COO
Robbie Robbins, EVP/Sr. Graphic Artist
Chris Ryall, Chief Creative Officer/Editor-in-Chief
Matthew Ruzicka, CPA, Chief Financial Officer
Alan Payne, VP of Sales
Dirk Wood, VP of Marketing
Lorelei Bunjes, VP of Digital Services

IDW founded by Ted Adams, Alex Garner,
Kris Oprisko, and Robbie Robbins

WINTERWORLD

By Chuck Dixon

COVER ART BY
Livio Ramondelli

SPOT ILLUSTRATIONS BY
Butch Guice and Tomas Giorello

EDITS BY
Justin Eisinger and Alonzo Simon

DESIGN BY
Richard Sheinaus/Gotham Design

WINTERWORLD

BOOK ONE

THE MECHANIC'S SONG

T HE WORLD HAS BEEN AS IT IS for as long as anyone alive can remember. No one living remembers what a summer breeze feels like. No one has felt a misting spring rain on their face. No one has seen leaves on the trees turn to the colors of the rainbow.

Winter is the only season now. Storms come and storms go with no attention to a calendar or the length of days. And between the storms the earth is an eternally frozen desert. No one knows why it all changed. A shift in the planet's orbit perhaps. Or perhaps the sun above us is dying. Or perhaps the world was always meant to go cold. Or it could be the fulfillment of a prophecy; the condemnation of an unseen god.

Dreaming of the past and looking for the causes of the endless ice that covers the planet are idle speculations and there is no time for such in this life. We are reduced to feeding off the remnants of what came before us. For fuel, for food, and for that rarest commodity of all, for warmth. Once the world teemed with life; plants and animals in an unimaginable profusion.

And man.

Men were everywhere and built great cities and roads and travelled across unlimited seas of open, unfrozen water. Now the human race is scattered, barely surviving in a hostile world that no longer welcomes it. In small bands and villages they survive day by day. We have returned to tribes and with them the suspicion of anyone strange and fear of what lies in the dark beyond the fire. Every solitary figure on the ice must be watched. Not for their intentions but to determine if they are real or not. If they are a mirage then they will pass. If they are human then we have seen into their heart and know their intentions.

They will take.

They will take our food.

They will take our warmth.

They will take whatever is left after that.

In the end, they will take our lives.

Every day is a fight for survival against the everlasting winter without and the hunger within.

My name is Scully and this is my world.

What a load of shit that was.

Perhaps.

I've never said perhaps in my whole goddamned life.

Wynn wanted me to tell her my story so she could write it down. She says it's important. Someday someone will read it and learn from it. I say someone will use the pages to start a fire or wipe their ass. It passes the time so I agree to talk while she writes.

"I'll do it," I told her, "so long as you write down what I say. Only what I say."

She promised she would, then I read it, and it's nothing like what I said. Maybe a little, sure. The words sound like those damned Flaubert novels she's always hunting for. She reads aloud to me during the long stretches so I know who wrote back then. Austen, Hugo, Tarkington. I like it better when she finds some Spillane or a James Bond book.

Wynn says she embellished my words. I say, if it's not my exact words then it's not my story. Write down what I say or to hell with it. Only what I say. She promises again. I guess kids are allowed second chances. I know I was. Some of the chances were given to me. Some I took. Some I wish I hadn't.

She wants to know about my past and this is how she's tricking me into talking about it. I tell her she won't like a lot of what she's going to hear. She says she can take it.

Here goes.

A ll that stuff before was mostly right.
I've never met anyone old enough who remembered the world back when it wasn't frozen all to hell. There was a really ancient guy once in a camp who said he saw the first year without a spring or summer. I think he was full of shit. I never called him on it. He'd tell stories of flying kites in the sky and running with his dog over green grass wearing nothing but short pants and how he had a dog who slept on the roof of his own doghouse. People would share some food with him to hear the stories. If that's how he got by then more power to him. I'd never do anything to take away another man's trade.

I do call myself Scully. I never told Wynn where I got that name. Maybe we'll get to that.

She's telling me to talk about what it was like when I was a kid.

I haven't thought of those times in a long time. Parts of it I haven't thought of since they happened to me. Most of it's not worth remembering. Some of it I'd rather not be reminded of.

We lived under the ice in a building in a place that was once by the ocean back when there was an ocean. It was a city once. Then the water rose and turned to ice a long time ago so most buildings were covered over and only the top floors of a few stuck up above the crust. We lived a few flights down in a place like that, hidden away in a sort of cave we made and insulated with blankets and other stuff we found.

It was just my family. My father, my mother and two younger kids. A boy and girl. They came after me so they were smaller. I only remember the youngest one being born. I don't know how old I was. Younger than Wynn by a few years. They were my family and the only people in the whole world I knew. Everyone else I saw were strangers and I only saw them from a distance. And, when I was lucky and smart and quick, they never saw me.

What were their names. I don't remember if they had names. Don't ask me.

We'd see other people, scavenging through the dead city just like us. We avoided them by staying out of sight when we could and running when we couldn't. Mostly they didn't want anything to do with us either. Sometimes they'd try to follow to find our hiding place. It was always my job to lead them away while the old man hid before heading home. Better to lose me than all our stuff. We'd seen other families after their hides had been found and they'd been turned out. Those that lived through the experience didn't last long. We'd find them out on the ice sooner or later froze to death or with their throats cut. More than a few times we'd find them quartered and gutted like game.

In this world, everyone's ass is up for grabs.

I'd find my way back on my own. I was out one time for three nights. Some strangers came through. A lot of them on sleds pulled by ponies. They had dogs. I led them on a chase through the ruins, climbing up hills of wreckage and squeezing through places the dogs couldn't follow. Killed one of the dogs. It was a smaller one that could press itself through the tight spaces I thought only I could wriggle through. The strangers gave up the hunt on the fourth day and sledded off.

The old man never came looking for me. Didn't do much to welcome me back either. Only told me that I'd forfeit the food I missed when I was out on the ice. I told him about how I fooled the strangers and even killed one of the dogs that was chasing me. He kicked me then and sent me out into the night to bring back the dog carcass. It took me most of that day to remember just where I left the dead dog. When I remembered the way all I found was a patch of red ice and some drag marks. Something found it before me and hauled it off to eat it. I hurried out of there and back to the warm hole we called home.

My reward was the worst beating of my life. The old man set into me with his fists and then his feet and I don't remember what after that.

I woke up to thin broth being ladled into my mouth. My mother was making sure I wasn't dead. She fed me to make me stronger. It had nothing to do with love. I carried my weight in the family and they relied on me for that until the other two kids were old enough to share the load. The old man wanted me back to scavenging and playing decoy for him. And she always did what he said. If she didn't he'd beat her too. He took after her with a steel rod one time just for taking a bigger piece of meat than him. That's what he said anyway. It wasn't like he needed much of an excuse to bat us around. She took a hit hard enough to make her ear bleed for days. She never could hear out of that ear again.

What did I do. Nothing, that's what I did. I watched him beat the hell out of her and listened to her screaming and begging. That's all she'd have done for me. And she lay there unconscious most of a day and he sat cradling her in his arms and crying about how sorry he was until it turned my stomach. I went out into the cold to get away from it.

He wasn't so sorry he didn't hit her again. He was only careful not to punch or kick her in the head. I took most of the beatings anyway even though I spent all of my time staying out of his way.

The old man had a rifle. An old bolt action job worn down to the bare metal. He kept that sucker oiled and clean. Took better care of it than he did his own woman and kids. It had a cracked wooden stock he bound with tape and wire. When he took it up on the ice it was wrapped in a woolen skin to keep the cold out of the metal. The old man told me that the metal of the barrel would crack from the sudden heat of the bullet if he let the steel get too cold. He told me we had to keep the rifle clean and warm. That was the only thing worth a damn he ever taught me.

There was a metal box of shells for it. Two dozen maybe. He'd oil and clean them too and keep the box close to his flesh under his layers of clothes. Every trip up onto the ice he'd take two bullets with him. He said one was for game and one was for me if I ever tried to run away. He'd smile like it was a joke. I knew better than that. His eyes told me otherwise. It was a joke for him not for me. For me it was purely a promise.

E very day was mostly the same unless we found a big cache of goods somewhere. Then we'd lay low for a while. Those days were rare and got even rarer as the years went on. Most days we found nothing.

Me and the old man would go up on the ice. We'd climb the twisting well of steel stairs up to the light and pull aside a barricade of old furniture. Some days there'd be snow banked up against the outside exit and we'd have to shovel our way clear.

I'd walk a ways ahead in case we ran into other scavengers. If they got close then I'd run like hell. I'd run in any direction away from the warm hole and where the old man was. A lot of times we saw other people doing what we were doing. They kept their distance. They lived near us, just like we were living. We didn't know what neighbor meant. They were strangers. They lived their lives within sight of us. They'd always be strangers.

Some we saw more than a few times. One was a trio of two men and what I thought was a boy my age. I saw them once in a while from a distance. Hard not to spot them with one of them wearing a yellow parka a blind man could see a mile away.

One time, I was in a hide watching them from closer than the old man would have cared for. I was lying under an opening in the eave of a rooftop watching the three cross an open area of snow between two buildings. The smallest, the one dressed in a yellow parka that was way too big, was trotting in the lead just like I would do. Looked to me like the dogs those strangers ran after me. That's what this kid was to the two men. A dog. Just like I was to the old man.

The dog kid was crouched at the base of a tall steel tower that rose out of the snow from somewhere below. It was a radio antenna. I know that now. The kid called out in a high voice and pulled a hood down so I could see long black hair. It was a girl. Probably about my age.

I held my breath and lay still to watch her. Her face was thin and pale. Her eyes were dark. I could see them when she took off the band of cloth she wore to protect them from the glare. The men plodded up to join her. They used the shovels they brought to dig down. I could tell they found something. They were talking fast and all excited. I wasn't close enough to hear the words.

From behind me I heard a hissing noise. It was the old man waving me back down to where he was standing. He was behind a high berm of drift snow and couldn't see what I could see. All he could hear was voices. He was waving and making sputtering noises and looking pissed as hell. I was lying two stories above him. A good twenty-foot drop. I knew he wouldn't risk climbing up to my perch. I just held up a hand to tell him to keep his mouth shut. He hissed between his teeth but didn't raise his voice to call out.

I turned back to see the men and girl had uncovered part of the antenna base. It was a section of rusted steel wall with a doorway in it. They worked to clear the snow and ice chunks away and yanked it open maybe a foot or so. They sent the girl in first. She squeezed in sideways and was gone.

There's no way to know how long I watched. The shadows got longer and deeper. The girl returned after a long while talking and laughing. She dug in the pockets of her coat and dropped stuff into the mittens of the waiting men. The stuff caught the light of the falling sun and sparkled red and gold. I started to belly crawl closer along the ledge to get a better look. My ankle was snagged on something. I looked back to see what hooked me. There was the old man gripping my leg in one fist and staring into my eyes with a silent promise of pure murder. This was a whole new level of rage for the old man. His face was red except for the white around his lips stretching over blackened teeth. He'd lost his shades in the climb. His eyes held mine so I could get a good look at just how dark his wrath was for me.

I defied him and he was going to make that as expensive as hell for me when we got back to our warm hole. He jerked me closer and whispered for me to follow him back down to the pack snow. We made our way down the narrow ledge back to a busted-out window I'd crawled out of and the old man had followed me through. He had the rifle slung over his back crossways. The ledge was slick with rime ice and when he went to stand to go through the window the barrel of the rifle caught on a tangle of wires. They were hanging down from the roof above. The tangle made him lose his footing for a second.

He went backwards off the ledge holding a hand out to me with a pathetic look on his face. I found that funny which only made him madder. He actually thought I'd take his hand. Thought I'd risk falling myself to save his sorry ass.

The old man fell hard on the pack ice. He tried to land on his feet and only wound up bending a leg under his weight. I could hear the wet crunch even through his layers of clothes and from twenty feet above him. He lay back and bit down on his mittened hand to keep the scream inside. I got down to him as fast as I could.

The old bastard lay on his back, face white with the pain from his leg. There were tears frozen on his lashes. I could see blood on his teeth where he bit right through the leather of his mitten and the wool gloves under that. I got him up on his feet and he leaned on me for support, one leg held clear. It was exhausting half-carrying him back to the warm hole. He weighed more than twice what I did. The worst was getting him down the stairs. He sat moaning on a sofa we used for the barricade while I rebuilt the heap of junk that hid the doorway to our place.

I called for my mother and she came up to help. We got him down the steps and into the hole. He howled like a snared fox as we got the coat off him. He howled louder when mother slit the pant leg off him with a skinning knife. There was a lot of blood there, frozen and flowing both. Two jagged ends of bone shone white where they ripped through his skin at the back of his calf. His eyes were red with the pain as mother and I grabbed his boot and jerked the bones back in place the best we could. He passed out as the twin rods retracted into the flesh. The two younger kids watched, not understanding but with eyes gleaming.

She wrapped the leg in the cleanest cloth we had. She told me to find something flat and straight and stiff to keep the leg straight. We burned every scrap of wood as we found it so there were no planks around. I went deeper in the building than I'd been before looking for anything like what mother had asked me for. It was dangerous down there. The weight of the ice had crushed in the walls in a lot of places. Ice moves like water only much, much slower. It is water after all. The pack ice was the only thing holding the structure up but it had buckled the floors below ours. The outside walls were collapsed where the tide of ice had punched through.

I lit my way with an oil lamp made from a glass bottle that once held something called Fanta. The flame on the cloth wick made the shadows dance and jump all around me as I moved. I used to tell myself stories about people that I imagined lived down here in the dark below us. They had no eyes or mouths and their skin was like oily leather. Even though the stories were just crap I made up in my head I was scared shitless that they were real and listening for me in the dark with their big flappy ears.

There was a heap of stuff littered all over the floor where a ceiling had collapsed. In the moldering clumps of plaster I found a strip of rusting steel with the word ACCOUNTING printed on it. It was about as long as my leg and a hand width across with two holes drilled in either end. Mother was pleased to see it when I got back. She strapped it on the old man's leg with my help. He grunted as the two of us used all of our strength to pull the bindings tight to hold the leg straight from above his knee to his ankle.

He passed out again and mother rested his head on a bundle of clothing. The old man was unconscious with a broken leg that would keep him immobile for a long time.

It was the happiest day of my life.

T he rifle was mine now.

It was the first time I ever touched it. I imagined that I could feel the power of it radiating through the sheepskin into the palms of my hands.

From here on it was up to me to go out on the scavenge alone. I was to take the rifle in case I ran into any caribou or ox or anything else worth shooting. I couldn't remember the last time that happened. But that was the purpose of the rifle. For the hunt.

The old man came around as I slid the metal tin of cartridges from under his shirt. He grabbed my wrist and tried to sit up. His eyes blazed into mine. I yanked the tin closer. He winced and released his grip to lie back with teeth clamped tight. I secured the tin under my own shirt and belted on my heavy coat.

"You lose that rifle and it's your hide," he said to me.

"I lose this rifle it means I'm dead. You better pray that don't happen or you're dead too," I said back.

He just glared at me letting me know I'd pay for those words.

Only I had the rifle now and maybe that wasn't true anymore.

Mother smiled and pressed a can of tinned fish into my hand.

"In case you get hungry on the scavenge," she said.

She'd never once showed me any kindness or concern. I had the rifle now. That meant I was the man. I was the one who had to be kept happy now. I was the one who decided if they ate or they didn't. I was the one who would bring back scrap to burn to keep them warm and oil to light the lair or let them shiver hungry in the dark.

"You know how to work that rifle," the old man said. The edge was gone from his voice.

"I watched you enough times. If you can clean it and load then I can too," I said.

He shut his eyes and turned his head as he lay back. I might have thought he was whipped. I might have thought he'd given in to the idea that he had given way to his own child. But I saw the furrow in his brow and the white lines around his mouth. As I turned away I caught the hard look from the corner of his eyes. Just in case I thought I'd gotten over on him, that one second-long look let me know I'd be paying dearly for this moment on the throne.

Dumb bastard looked angry when he should have looked scared.

I pulled up my hood and knotted it. I slid my goggles on my nose and took the rifle up the steps toward the light. The old man, the woman who called herself my mother, and my sister and brother watched me go without a word.

wasn't used to being out on my own.

I'd been up on the ice alone before. This was the first time I was on my own and no one telling me what to do or where to go or what to bring back. The only time I wasn't running from strangers to draw them far from our hide. The only time I was up here with only me telling me where to go and what to do.

And I knew right where I was going. I laid awake all night thinking of it.

I made my way back to those building tops and climbed the high berm of snow and lay down atop it, the rifle in my fists. I scanned the ground from the crest of that drift watching for movement out on the open white. I watched that antenna tower too. Most of all I watched the furrow of snow dug away from its base and that corrugated door now braced shut with a steel bar wedged against it. I watched for a long time to be sure.

I slid down the opposite slope of the berm on my back, dropping to a crouch at the bottom. Nothing moved on the horizon. I scooted closer to the base of the tower trotting low like a wolf would. The front sight of the rifle swung back and forth before me as I loped along.

More snow and ice had been cleared from the doorway than before. It looked like they spent time making sure the doorway could swing all the way open to let the grown men inside. There were lots of boot prints in the loose snow here. They led away back where I'd seen the two men and the girl come from. There were more prints than just three people would make. They'd brought others back with them to loot more of the shiny things that had me so curious.

Maybe they'd already taken all that there was. If that were so then why did they brace the door shut like that. It wouldn't keep anyone out but it would keep the snow from drifting inside and filling the corrugated shack at the base of the antenna tower. That meant they planned to come back. That meant there was more to scavenge inside. And I was burning to find out what was in there that made them so goddamned happy.

I moved quick over the open snow and rolled myself into the furrow before the door. I busted the ice away from the base of the bar with the butt of the rifle and pulled the bar clear. The door opened easy and I ducked inside pulling it shut behind me. Maybe anyone who came along would think the bar fell aside on its own. I didn't care. I was high on the freedom to explore on my own without the old man up my ass about every little thing. For the first time in my life I wasn't thinking every second about how to keep him pleased enough not to kick the shit out me.

It was dark inside the metal shed and smelled like old rust and fresh piss. I dug out a soda bottle lamp and pulled off a mitten with my teeth to check to see if the wick was wet with oil. I struck a precious match on the rough surface of a steel beam to light the wick.

The bottle held high in one hand the rifle trained from the hip in the other, I moved across the shed past the network of steel uprights that rose from where they were bolted into the floor to form the base of the antenna tower. Beyond them I found a heavier steel door that leaned in a broken frame. I squeezed through the gap and found that I was on a landing at the top of a stairwell. The guttering lamp showed the gleam of rime ice on the steps. I moved cautiously down the steps with the rifle shoulder slung and a hand on a tube steel railing. The railing was clear of ice. The others who had been here rubbed it clean as they descended into the dark just as I was doing. I saw the treads of their boots in the rime along the railing wall. Sets of prints going down and coming back up. They'd made a trip or two since I saw them last. They were gone now. I'd follow their trail down to the treasure.

I thought about the girl as I moved lower and lower down the stairwell following the boot prints. If I'm being honest, and you made me promise to be honest, I thought about that girl more than what I might find at the bottom of these stairs. I lay awake thinking of her hair and her eyes. She was too far for me to really see her clearly but I had a picture of her in my mind. She was pretty with thick eyelashes and a long clean neck and smooth hands and she smelled nice.

Don't laugh at me. How the hell should I know what she'd smell like. The best thing I ever smelled was canned peaches thawing by the fire. Maybe I thought she smelled like sweet peaches.

Sure, I had what you'd call a fantasy, I guess. I'd get to the bottom of the steps and she'd be there waiting for me. Or maybe she was in trouble and I could get her out of it. Maybe a wolf or a rabid dog had her trapped or maybe her ankle was caught some way and she couldn't free it. I'd rescue her and she'd be so happy and so nice and she'd beg me to take her with me. I didn't have the rest of the make-believe worked out past that. I didn't even know what was making me think that way. Sure, I know now what was going on with me. I had maybe three hairs on my balls back then and was still working it all out.

I went down deeper than I'd ever gone before in any ruin. The walls of the stairwell were concrete block reinforced with steel beams. They were cracked in places and I could see where water had come through then frozen in thick ropes of black ice. There was nothing to make me think the place wasn't solid, more solid than the building I called home anyway. The girl and others had made their way up and down this way more than once so I felt pretty safe.

The boot prints led across a landing where a heavy steel door was propped open. There was at least another flight down from here but the prints led this way. The treasure lay somewhere on this level where the boot prints ended.

A corridor led past doorways and turned finally out into a large area. It was too big for my bottle lantern to reach the walls or ceiling. It was one big open room, the largest enclosed area I'd ever seen in my life up to then. There were rows of steel racks; some upright and some lying on their sides. There were heaps of clothing strewn about the floor. I poked a boot toe at one of them. It was frozen clumps long ago welded to the floor by ice.

I held the lantern low to follow the boot prints clearly showing on the rime that covered a smooth uniform surface. It was tile. I'd never seen a tile floor before. It was slick under the dusting of ice and I made sure of my footing as I followed the tracks deeper into the dark. I ducked under a banner that hung canted from the ceiling.

It had big letters on it that read, WINTER WHITE SALE.

Funny, right.

The lantern light bounced back at me and I crouched low, unslinging the rifle before I realized it was my own light reflected back at me by sheets of glass. I moved closer and set the lantern down on a glass counter top. The sloped pane at the front of the counter was broken out with only a few jagged blades of glass poking from the frame. Within the case lay trays that still held some of the same gleaming gems I'd seen the girl drop into the hands of the men she was with. There were more scattered over the floor.

I pulled a mitten free with my teeth. I reached in and picked a few remaining pieces from the corner of a tray. They made a crinkling noise. They were small discs as big around as a deer's eye. In the lantern light they gleamed back green and red and orange. The crinkling was come kind of tinted paper. I unwrapped it and sniffed at the disc inside then touched my tongue to it.

It was sweet, almost painfully sweet. I put the whole thing in my mouth and it began to melt. My first piece of candy. Butterscotch. I remember it better than my first drink. Better than I want to remember my first woman. I let the rich nectar fill my mouth and swallowed. Then I began scooping up all that remained of the hard candies from the inside of the counter and from the floor. I stuffed my pockets full and looked around for any kind of sack or box I could find to carry more. My search took me deeper into the gloom, the lantern raised high to the wonders of this Aladdin's cave.

I was looking high instead of low when I stumbled over something in the middle of the aisle and went down hard on the tiles. The lantern skidded away out of reach but I held onto the rifle. I got to my feet and found the lantern. It was still lighted and the glass had not broken. I walked back to see what I stumbled over.

It was a man. He lay on his back with his throat slit ear-to-ear in a black pool of ice. His eyes were wide open and white with frost made by his own tears. I didn't recognize the face but I knew the parka. Forest green with patches of silvery duct tape where it had been repaired many times. I raised the lantern high and found a second humped figure lying on its side a ways further along the aisle. This man wore a red-and-black scarf about his neck and a black coat over white down coveralls. There was a black puckered hole just above his nose. The back of his skull was gone and clumps of his brain shone pearly white against the ebon ice of his own blood.

I was shaking, the barrel of the rifle wavering before me, as I moved further along the aisle. I found the yellow parka thrown to the floor. Then a sweater that looked like someone had taken a knife to it though there was no blood. After that a pair of quilted pants with the cinch belt cut away. There were black skid marks on the tile and signs of someone being dragged through the ice. I stood holding my breath and listening with eyes pressed shut.

I couldn't hear anything but the beating of my own heart and I willed that to slow down as I stood with the dark all around. I listened as hard as I could because I knew I couldn't go looking any more. I didn't want to see what I knew I might see. I didn't want to follow those black heel marks any further into the dark.

Not if all I'd find is what I knew I'd find.

Me and the old man had found women's bodies before on the ice. We'd seen how they'd been used.

The silence was total. It was complete. I was as alone as I would have been on the surface of the moon.

I retraced my steps and picked the yellow parka up off the floor. I set the rifle and lantern down on a counter top. The parka had the word Aspen stitched on the breast in fancy script. I shucked out of my ragged old coat and slipped the parka on. I recalled it had been plenty big on the girl. It fit me just fine with plenty of room in the shoulders. She was smaller than me. I lifted the collar to my nose and sniffed. It smelled of grease and sweat and something else. Something as sweet as peaches but not peaches.

I picked up the rifle and lantern and made my way back to the surface. It was full-on dark and the moon shimmered down through the low clouds with a muted glow. The whole world was silver and gray below it. Before me, up out of the furrow at the base of the antenna, two sets of tracks led away black against the sylvan snow. One led back to the warm hole. The other to the men I followed down into the dark and back into the light.

I stood there the longest time before I realized that I'd left all that sweet candy down below in the pockets of my old coat.

I knew where to find even more.

T he tracks were easy to follow even in the dark. The strangers were pulling something behind them leaving a pair of drag marks.

I kept to the shadows cast by walls where I could. I hugged drifts and crawled along slow past buildings with fires glowing in them. Some scrounged by night. The shadows could hide them as much as me. I watched the dark for traces of vapor that would let me know someone was waiting there.

The boot tracks and drag marks went around the fires inside the buildings too. Whoever these guys were they were avoiding a stand-up fight with anyone who might have greater numbers than them.

The trail moved around the half-moon wall of the top levels of a big stadium building sticking out of the ice. The old man and me had scavenged around here a few times. It had been picked clean a long while back. I found stacks of some kind of magazines with pictures of what went on here back in the days. Sunny days and smiling people and big men in colorful outfits with numbers on them. More people than I'd ever seen in my life would pack into places like this to watch guys running around and throwing a ball to one another.

The magazines had rows of pictures of the men with their names underneath. Some smiled up at me from the pages like they wanted to be my friend. Others glared like I was their worst enemy.

Whatever happened here was important to everyone back then. Me, I can't imagine sitting out in the open to watch anything. I guess they had ways to keep warm. I still can't imagine anyone wanting to watch someone else play a game.

I followed the tracks to where they entered a wide gap in the wall where it had collapsed. The tracks climbed high drifts that blocked the gap. I couldn't follow them directly. That would mean skylining myself at the top of the drift. Even by night my silhouette would be plain against the moon-backed clouds. The owners of those boots could be anywhere on the other side.

Instead I trotted along the base of the stadium ring until I came to a place where the wall had been parted by some tremor that happened years and years before. The ice shifts all the time, you know. It's maybe earthquakes down below. Maybe it's just the plates of pack ice rubbing together. The pressure builds up and something has to give. The world man left behind was being slowly crushed between giant jaws of ice.

The break in the wall was just wide enough across to let me through. I came out inside the stadium. I moved along a terrace to where I could see down into the shallow bowl of the place. The curving walls all around were terraced in snow drifts that clung to the benches where people once sat in thousands and thousands to watch the colorful men who smiled and glared.

Down on a flat area in the center of the oblong walls was a motor. A machine. It was a big one with wheels as tall as me in the front and big steel treads in the back. It had a shell of angled steel painted white in some places, gray in others, and rusted metal showing through the chipped paint. A thin line of exhaust rose from a standpipe at the back of it. I could feel the rumble of its idling engine even as far away as I was.

This was the closest I'd ever been to a motor. I'd seen them moving way out on the Big Ice, just little black specks moving past in the far distance heading for where I did not know. Sometimes at night we'd see lights moving over the flat sheet of ice. None had ever turned our way in my memory.

I'd lay awake thinking about what kind of people were in them and where they were going and wondering what the machines were and what made them work. The magazines we found sometimes had pictures of motors all shiny and new and happy people sitting in them or standing by them in green parks and in front of immaculate houses and parked on sandy beaches with endless open water lapping the shore. I'd look at them sometimes before feeding them into the fire.

This machine had nothing in common with those pictures. It looked hard and brutal like the men who made it move. Those men were warm inside and enjoying the goods they'd looted. I saw a sled outside the motor where the drag marks ended. It was empty now. From the depth of the tracks I knew it was heavy with scavenge when they dragged it here. I squinted hard and could see a yellowish glow through the narrow gaps of closed slats down the side of the vehicle.

They pulled in here out of the worst of the wind through a broad opening at the far end of the stadium. The deep gouges made by the wheels and treads had not filled in with snow. I gauged that they'd been here a day or two but no more. They'd come since the last heavy snow fall. The wind was slowly filling in the tracks they left behind them.

By my count there were at least three of them. I could tell that much by studying their boot prints. They were grown men. I knew that much from the length of their strides. You learn stuff like that over time. You can't help it if you're paying attention.

There could be any number more inside the machine.

I'd have to wait and watch to know for sure how many more there were.

I picked a spot on the highest shelf of the stadium. There was a kind of shelter there with a glass wall at the front of it facing the inside of the bowl. Some of the glass was missing but I'd be out of the worst of the wind.

It was a long cold night I spent huddled on a high bench in a corner of the booth. I found a thick plastic banner about ten feet long and five feet wide and wrapped myself in it to cut the wind. I dug inside my clothes to where the tin of fish lay warm against my skin. I opened it with my knife and ate half the can with my fingers. Then I washed it down with water from the jug I also kept next to my skin so it would stay thawed. My mouth tasted oily and fishy no matter how many times I ran my tongue over my teeth. I stuck my hands in the pockets of the yellow parka and felt something there. Some of those hard candies were down in the lining where they fell through holes in the pockets. I unwrapped one and sucked on it. It washed the fishy taste from my mouth. The flavor of it almost made me dizzy with the sweetness. Then I remembered that this candy was put here by the girl. She meant this for herself. She'd be having this candy now instead of me. She'd be alive now if not for what happened.

I didn't want to think about that. There was a lot I didn't want to think about. Like, why was I here. Why wasn't I back in the warm hole where I belonged. Why'd I take her coat and leave my own behind all filled with more of this candy. The old man and mother and the other kids would sure love some candy only I hadn't thought of them. Not one time. I hadn't thought of anything but following these men ever since I found those quilted pants sliced open with knives like the skin peeled from an animal.

What was that girl to me. I didn't know her. She'd never even seen me and might just have spit on me if she did. Everything I knew about her I made up in my head while I should have been sleeping. I'd have been better off if I'd forgotten her, better off if I went back to the warm hole and never thought of her again.

I knew that wasn't going to happen. I wasn't going to forget her. I wasn't even going to try. And if I walked away now I'd always remember the men who were the last ones to see her alive. I'd always remember, or what I imagined I'd remember, what they did to her before she died. My last memory of her would always be her throwing candy into the hands of the two men she was with. I don't know if I actually heard her laugh when she did that. Memory is funny. I can swear I heard her make a high musical happy sound, happy at what she'd discovered deep down in that dark store. I can hear it now like I believe I heard it then. She was happy. That's the memory I have of her. And, as crazy and stupid as it sounds, I felt like I knew her. That means I felt like they'd done what they'd done to one of my own and I was going to make it right.

What the hell made me think that way. I'd never given a damn about anything or anyone. Long as I can remember it I've found plenty of dead folks on the ice. Men and women and kids too. Some just frozen bundles lying in drifts. Others torn up by animals and pieces carried off. At least I hoped it was animals though I know better now. And none of them meant a damn to me. If I had any feelings at all it was that it was better it happened to them than to me. In fact, I had nothing but contempt for anyone dumb enough to let the cold get to them. Death was for the stupid and he'd never catch me. I'd never make the kind of mistakes that would lead to me being just another lonely lump of rags in the snow.

And there I was, nothing more than a kid, with a rifle I'd never even fired in my life, ready to take on how many grown men for some nameless girl who'd never know anyone cared enough to try and get even for her.

Death had found another idiot for his list.

T urned out there were only three of them after all.

I set up to watch the machine from a hide on a level above them. I scooped out snow from under one of the metal benches and covered myself over with that plastic banner. I'm not saying it was cozy but I was out of the wind, conserving my heat. From there I could see the whole floor of the stadium without being seen myself. I held the rifle close to my body to keep the action warm and locked an eye on the machine and listened to the soft thrumming purr of its engine.

Guess I dozed off a bit. I came awake when I heard metal on metal.

They were animals but they weren't so far gone as to shit where they lived. I took note and kept count as, one by one over the course of the day, they climbed out of the roof hatch to walk a distance from the machine to squat in the snow.

They were three. The biggest wore a blue and white toque on his head with a silly ring-tailed tassel with a fuzzy pom-pom on the end hanging down his back. Another had a dark brown parka fringed with wolf fur around the hood and full face woolen mask pulled down on his head. The last wore heavy padded overalls in faded red with a sheep-shearling vest tied closed with wire loops. His head was bare except for a wooly bush of hair and a long matted beard streaked with gray. One at a time as the shadows crept over the stadium floor they hurried out of the shelter of the machine to take a piss or bare their asses to leave a load before shuffling back. The bearded guy was out most often and made angry noises as he squirted watery shit that steamed where it landed. He ran back with knees wide apart and ass burning from whatever was troubling his gut.

He was the weakest. Whatever I did had to start with him.

Remember, I'd never fired the rifle before. I'd watched the old man load it and clean it and make sure it was oiled. I recalled seeing him actually shoot the damn thing maybe two times. Once when he missed a rabbit on the hop and once when he winged a caribou that we spent a whole day running down only to have to give it up to a bear that claimed the carcass by the time we reached it.

The best plan, as I saw it, was to get as close as I could get. I'd get so close there was no way I could miss. That wasn't going to be easy with the machine in the middle of the stadium and surrounded all around by empty white.

It snowed steady all morning and afternoon. It covered my hide in a blanket of fresh powder. I crawled from under the banner leaving it in place in case I wanted to return after dark.

I worked my way around the curve of the stadium keeping an eye locked on the machine. There was no way to tell if they were blind in there or not. As far as I knew they were watching me the whole time. The best plan was to work in close as I could but not so close I couldn't outrun them if that hatch came open in a hurry. They'd be in there all cozy and enjoying whatever loot they dragged back. That wouldn't last forever. They could power up and leave at any time so I couldn't afford to wait any longer.

Thinking back, I have to wonder what the hell was in my head. I must have been half crazy to think I could take on three grown men, mean ones at that, all on my own. I know now that it started with me being pissed off at what they'd done. That changed when I saw the machine. If I could take them and own that monster for myself. Well, that would be the biggest scavenge of them all.

But I didn't forget the laughing girl in the yellow parka. I didn't let go of that rage. I kept it banked inside me like the embers of a fire I didn't want to go out. That was a fire I needed to give me what I'd need for what happened next. You can call it courage. I'm not sure what it was but I knew I'd have to have it down there inside if I was going to kill a man.

Or three.

I was down level with the machine and moving along the curve to a place that still offered some cover. I cursed myself for trading my drab old coat for this bright yellow parka that showed up against the snow like I was waving a flag.

A metallic clang let me know someone was exiting the machine. I dove behind a hump of drift that was poor cover but my only choice within range. The biggest guy in the silly cap climbed up grunting and coughing with an ugly dry hack. The tail of his cap bobbled behind him. I was close enough to hear someone speaking from inside. They sounded angry. The big guy barked back telling them to stick it up their ass. Unlike other times when they exited the machine, this time the big guy left the hatch open. I could see the glow of light shifting in the wave of air rising from inside. It was warm in there.

Levered up just enough to keep one eye over the hump of the drift, I saw that he didn't climb down the ladder to the ground. He moved with care along the top of the machine toward the rear where he crouched over the standpipe. It was covered over now by the new snowfall that made a roof of white over the whole machine. The man grunted and batted at the snow with his mittens and cleared the top of the pipe. A thick puff of gray smoke belched up into his face and he coughed and cursed some more. The man stood and kicked the rest of the drift away from the standpipe which was now leaking a steady stream of hot exhaust into the thin air. It drifted down the side of the machine in a dirty cloud to be carried over the top of the snow crust. The oily stink of it reached me where I was lying behind the drift without moving. I watched the big guy huff and puff and jam himself back down into that hatch. He left the hatch levered open and I could hear them bitching at one another but not clear enough to hear what they were saying.

I lay there shivering, afraid to move in case one of them popped his head up to see something in bright yellow scuttling over the snow near their ride. I watched the quavering air rising from the opening and wondered why they'd let so much of their precious heat waste away like that. I wished I could climb up there and hold my hands over it for just a little bit. There had to be a reason they were doing that and I knew I'd be able to figure it out if I weren't so goddamned cold.

After a while, almost at full dark, a hand reached up and yanked a handle to drop the hatch closed with a bang. Hurting all over from the cold that had leeched into my muscles, I rose up and stumbled back up to my hide. I crawled in under the banner. I was covered over by a foot of snow. That was good. Snow would insulate me. I peeled down as much as I could despite the cold and rubbed at my arms and legs until the feeling came back. I unlaced my boots and rubbed at the layers of frayed socks until my toes burned with the returned circulation. I put the layers back on and re-strapped the boots tight before a meal of frozen fish I had to thaw in my mouth. I warmed the cold water from my jug in my mouth as best I could before swallowing. Two candies for dessert then I was ready for what came next.

The bearded guy with the trots wasn't their only weakness. Everything that lives has to eat, piss, shit and breathe.

That last one was going to cost them.

T he best strategy still began with the hairy shitter.

They were deaf and blind in there; I could see lights showing dimly through the slits of the view ports along the front. They wouldn't be able to see shit now as they were night blind.

I moved up on the machine in the dark close enough to put a mittened hand on the armored side. I could feel the power of it vibrating through the steel shell and into my fingers, up my arm and resounding through my whole body. It was like a sleeping monster and I almost forgot the danger I was in as I wondered at how it worked and what made it go and what it was like inside.

The scrape of metal on metal broke the spell. Someone was undogging the hatch above me. I dropped and rolled under the machine making a furrow in the bank of snow that had drifted up against the side. I could hear loud voices over the hum of the motor. No way to tell if they were arguing or just having one damned loud conversation. The hatch banged shut, cutting off the voices to silence. I crawled on my belly and watched through the gap my body made in the drift. The scrape of boots on the rungs reached me. One boot left the ladder then another and a man walked away through the snow. It was the wooly-headed man with the liquid guts.

The man was totally night blind, as I thought. He didn't see my tracks in the fresh snow. If he did he could follow them right to where I was hiding.

He was squatting bare-assed and facing away from me whinnying with pain as a stinking stream sprayed from his ass and onto the snow with a wet trumpeting sound.

Maybe he sensed me behind him or saw a shadow from the corner of his eye. He turned to me with eyes wide and staring from inside that bush of frizzled hair. The last thing in the whole damned world he expected to see was a kid holding a rifle on him from almost near enough to touch. In turning he lost his balance and fell to his knees and one hand. I couldn't see the other hand with his body in the way.

His eyes were locked on mine. I matched his gaze as I slowly shook my head. I'd have spoken a warning to him but I was holding two cartridges clamped tight between my lips to keep them warm and handy. I raised the barrel sights to train them on his head. I fought down the shivers to keep the rifle steady.

The lines around his eyes crinkled. That's the only way I knew that he was smiling as the thick mat of fuzz on his face hid any further expression.

"I know that coat," he said.

I said nothing.

"She your sister," he said.

I said nothing but shifted from his eyes to see his shoulder dipping slow as could be. He was moving that hand I couldn't see to reach for something.

"What was she to you," he said with his voice rising.

I still couldn't see his other hand.

"Was she your sweetheart."

I don't remember giving the trigger that last ounce of pressure.

The bullet took him somewhere through that thatch of beard. His throat. His mouth. I'll never know. A shower of blood burst from his face and I saw slimy gray bits go skittering over the crust of snow behind him, carried on a red spray. He sighed then and slowly slumped to the snow as if laying down for a nap.

I killed a man. It meant no more to me than crushing a lice I'd found in my hair.

Not right then anyway.

The sound of the rifle was the loudest thing I'd ever heard in my life. It was bouncing back at me from the stadium walls, echo after echo after echo. I turned with the rifle to the machine and held the front tangs of the sight aimed toward the closed hatch. I waited for someone to raise it up to see what that explosion was all about. I'd put a bullet through their skull or at least make them drop away.

Nothing happened. No one responded. The machine just purred away like before.

I moved the two cartridges between my lips, tasting the bitter copper taste of the jackets. I realized then that the rifle had an expended shell in it. I quickly jerked the bolt open ejecting the spent round and inserted a new one and jacked it home. I ran to the machine and climbed the ladder to the top. They'd be expecting their friend to be coming back sometime. There was one chance and only a little time to make my idea work.

I reached the top of the machine and hurried to sit down on the hatch door to study it. If they wised up to what was happening my weight on the door would buy me a few seconds. I knew that if they both put their minds to it then one skinny kid wouldn't stop them levering the hatch open for long. I spun on my ass looking over the door with rising panic. There were no levers or bolts or handles. The door was built to be operated from the inside. There had to be a way to secure it shut from the outside if I could only think of it.

I could feel a new vibration through the soles of my boots. A rhythmic clumping sound. Someone climbing the rungs of a ladder to reach the hatch from the inside.

could feel through the seat of my pants someone working the latch back and forth. They'd be pushing up in a second to find the hatch was weighted down by something. Tears started in my eyes and froze there on my lashes. I spun my sight around everywhere looking for a way to keep that hatch secured in place.

Directly across from the place where it hinged open there was a hasp sort of deal. It was a steel nose on the hatch set so it secured between two protrusions coming off the circular frame. Through the hasp was drilled a hole for a lock of some sort, I guess. I pulled the rifle back to slide under my arm and drew the cleaning rod from the end of the stock where it set in a well under the barrel. Through my ass I was feeling the drumming vibration of someone pounding on the hatch from within. It was a sharp impact. They were using a tool or the butt end of a weapon.

I leaned forward and ran the cleaning rod through the hole through the hasp. It was tempered steel and fit snug. I tapped the cap on the end of the two-foot rod with the rifle stock until I'd hammered it through the holes, leaving equal lengths of the rod sticking from either end. It would hold for now.

Standing up from the hatch with wobbly legs I made my way back to the standpipe. I pulled my mittens from my pocket where I'd put them earlier to leave my fingers free to work the rifle. I pushed one and then the other mitten down into the open mouth of the pipe. I upended the rifle to use the barrel to tamp the mittens down into the pipe until they plugged it completely. Nothing escaped the end of the pipe now. I took my gloved hands and placed them around the barrel of the pipe to enjoy the heat radiating from the metal. The engine below rumbled on, muted now with its mouth blocked by my mittens.

They kept the standpipe clear for a reason. It took me a bit to figure out why that was important and why they kept the top hatch open so long. If that pipe was blocked then that greasy smoke that came from it had nowhere to go. Wouldn't take long for the machine to fill up with that poison air. That's how I reasoned it anyway. Same as we had to have a way to let the smoke out of the warm hole, these bastards had to be able to vent their machine.

My fingers thawed finally and I took them from the hot pipe and put them under my arms. I returned to the hatch and sat down on top of it. I sat there with the rifle hugged close to my body. Through the hatch I could feel hammering from below for a while. Then it went quiet. I moved to lay on the hatch and pulled my hood clear of my ear to press it to the metal dome.

There was a scraping sound coming through the surface. I leapt back as a painful ringing sound struck my ear. I went down on my ass and watched the hatch juddering slightly in the frame. The hasp was jiggling causing the steel cleaning rod to shiver either end with a twanging sound. I laid my gloved hands on the hatch. I could feel a series of sharp impacts from below. They were banging on something below that, in turn, was working as a wedge on the underside of the hatchway. The hatch was thrumming with each blow. Flecks of old paint were popping off the frame with every strike. The cleaning rod wasn't vibrating any more as it was no longer true through the hatch. The force from below had bent it in the hasp and forced the ends down. The lip of the hatch was rising above the throat of the opening bit by tiny bit.

I stood up then and backed from the hatch with my rifle trained on the opening. There was no running away now. No backing down. If those bastards were coming out it would be one at a time. They'd have to expose themselves to a bullet in the skull. All I had to do was outlast them.

Maybe they thought of that about the same time. Maybe they thought they had a better idea. The hammering stopped from below. The hatch rested back down tight in the opening.

The engine roared then louder than before. The machine jolted under me and I fell back hard. I let go of the rifle to steady myself and find a hand hold. It tumbled off to fall into the snow. I thought at first the rifle was sliding away behind me. It was the machine moving. The bastards got it into gear and floored it to break out of the ice clinging to the treads and tires. I slid across the roof until I fetched up against the base of an antenna mast. There was a steel handhold within reach and I locked my fingers around it and braced my boot on the base of the mast.

The machine took off across the floor of the stadium jinking and sliding all over. I was thumped hard on the roof. It felt like my arm was going to be yanked out of the socket. I held on anyway. If they threw me off I'd break something for sure. Or maybe I'd be crushed to jelly under those monster wheels.

They hit a drift. The front end of the machine went airborne. The wheels crashed down on the other side and I lost my hold. Tumbling toward the front end I recalled that I still had that last cartridge in my mouth. I spit it out as my elbow cracked on some part of the bulkhead sending a pain like an electric shock into my chest. I smacked my face hard off the roof. The air filled with swirling black specks.

The engine died then with a series of dry clunks. The mighty rumble went dead silent. The machine settled down on the drift at an angle. A cloud of vapor rose from the vents above the motor compartment at the rear. The bitter tang of hot steel drifted over me. I got to my knees and crawled along the slanted angle of the roof. I threw my weight down on the hatch. I gripped the rung of a handhold on one side and dug my fingers into the recess of a shallow dent on the other. They might get this lid open but they were going to have to fight to get it done.

lay there a long time. I either dozed off or passed out. When I came to there was the first glimmer of milky gray light along the horizon. The sun was rising invisible behind the shelter of clouds.

I laid my ear to the hatch and heard nothing. No voices or banging. There was no movement. No sense of life.

Coming up on my knees I felt dizzy but fought it down. My muscles were stiff. The chill felt like it reached my bones. If I stayed exposed here and unmoving the cold would kill me. As much as every movement brought pain, I belly crawled to the ladder. I lowered myself to the snow one rung at a time and hobbled back for my rifle.

It lay ruined in the snow. The stock was splinters and the barrel was bent at the middle. The machine had run over it when they were trying to buck me off.

I looked to the machine. It was still sitting athwart the drift like a dead thing. The lights inside were out. I turned to look around the stadium. The body of the bearded man lay where it had fallen. I trotted over and used the toe of my boot to lever the man onto his back and search through his clothes. There in an inside pocket next to his chest I found what he'd been reaching for. A six-shot revolver with a short, nasty barrel. I recognized it for a gun but had never seen one like it. I stood keeping the dead machine in my sight while I worked out how the weapon functioned. I finally managed to work the hammer back using the edge of my hand. In trying to maintain a grip my finger pulled the trigger home and the revolver went off with a sound that startled me. A bullet kicked up a gout of snow at my feet.

Drawing the hammer back more deliberately this time, and with my fingers on the outside of the trigger guard, I re-charged the weapon. I carefully, slowly, lowered the hammer on a live round. Then I moved back to the machine keeping it raised in one hand before me.

It was an ordeal climbing that ladder again. There wasn't an inch of my body that didn't ache. And I could feel my right eye swelling shut where my face struck the armor shell of the machine earlier. I knelt at the hatch and hammered on the metal with the butt of the revolver. No answer from inside. I worked to remove the cleaning rod from the hasp and it was hard work. As much as I worried that the bitch wouldn't hold the night before now it was wedged in there too tight to budge.

Pulling and pushing on one end of the rod I slowly weakened the stressed metal until it snapped clean off. I prized the free end from the hasp and sat back. I held the revolver trained on the gap as I raised the hatch cover up with my free hand. There was a scrape and a loud thump as it hinged wide and dropped open. I jerked back, the revolver extended in both hands now. The inside of the hatch was gouged with a broad strip of bared white metal where the finish had been violently scraped away.

Taking my sweet time I leaned out over the opening, holding the revolver down into the dark. The sickening stench of fresh vomit rose to meet me. I dry gagged, my empty stomach turning on itself. I gave my eyes time to adjust. Down below I could see a long metal bar leaning at an angle below the hatch well. It was the wedge they had jammed against the door from the inside. A heavy mallet lay on the decking. They were hoping to force the hatch by hammering their wedge upright. That was their plan before they switched to trying to buck me off.

"You sons of bitches hear me. Any of you alive in there." I shouted down. The effect was spoiled when my voice cracked.

I made spit in my mouth and fought to swallow it down.

"You speak up now or I'll make it hard for you. I will, I swear," I said.

Hell, I wouldn't have scared anybody. I was using up all the scared. There wasn't enough left for anybody else.

I set a foot on the first rung inside the hatch and twisted at an awkward position to keep the gun aimed down into the dark. By the third rung I smelled something under the stink of puke. It was making me gag. I felt my throat closing. It was a greasy, oily reek that was pure poison. I clambered out of there and lay retching atop the machine and spat out an oily mix that was all my guts could manage.

I moved forward of the hatch and sat looking at the open hatch. I could see it now, a discoloration in the air rising up out of the port. It came up on the heat from within. I sucked on a hard candy and waited for the chemical fog to drift up and away before I'd try to re-enter.

The sun was falling before I tried again. I crawled to the edge of the opening and sniffed. Still stank of vomit and shit. But the greasy taste was mostly out of the air. And there for damned sure wasn't anyone alive down there.

kept the revolver pointed before me as I climbed down enough to drop into the body of the machine.

The throat of the hatch gave way to an open compartment. Enough light came through the slits in the vents to let me find my way forward. The vents were backed by some kind of clear material with a mesh of fine wire embedded in it. There were a pair of hatches set forward but they'd been welded shut either by the current owners or whoever they stole it from.

That left only the top hatch for ventilation. It trapped the heat in and kept the cold and the curious out. It also turned the place into a death trap as the diesel exhaust had nowhere to escape to once I blocked the exhaust with my mittens. I understand, looking back, that I killed these assholes with carbon monoxide. At the time I was thinking of the machine as an animal. I knew it had to breathe.

The two assholes were up front at the driver controls. They went out in a bad way. Eyes bulging. Mouths swollen with their own black tongues. Pants filled with their own shit. Vomit spattered all around. One of them had a flat black pistol in his fist. Maybe he wanted to kill himself to escape the pain of strangling on poisoned air. His time ran out before he worked up the nerve to put a bullet in his own head.

Well, to hell with him. To hell with both of them. Nobody offered that poor black-haired girl a better way out.

I climbed back up top and fished my mittens out of the exhaust pipe. That opened up a draught inside the machine. The vents over the engine housing whistled as air was sucked into the vacuum created there by the choking motor.

Returning below I found an electric lamp and worked a switch to light it up. I explored the rear cargo area. It was a mess of stacked plastic containers holding a jumble of canned goods, clothes of all kinds, magazines filled with pictures of naked women, plastic jugs of water, bottles of liquor that were mostly empty and assorted boxes of ammunition in all kinds of sizes. None of it was stored in any order. It was all thrown in with other worthless junk like moldy stuffed animal toys and parts to what might have been radios or some other kind of electronics I had no way of recognizing then.

Strapped against one wall of the compartment was what I knew was a motorcycle. I'd seen them in the same magazines where I'd seen cars. It was battered and streaked with rust but the cables and hoses on it looked glossy and new. The tires were studded with spikes. Someone cared for it. Maybe one of the assholes I gassed. Well, it was mine now. In fact, the whole damned machine was mine if I only I knew what to do with it. As far as I knew I'd killed it forever.

I found a plastic bucket with a sealed top. The faded paper picture pasted to the side showed a steaming bowl of white tubes covered in a steaming orange mess of some kind. I pried it open to find it was filled with little curled tubes. I nibbled the end of one. It was dry and turned to a paste in my mouth as I chewed it. It was bland but edible. There was a clear plastic pack of yellow powder in the tub. I tore open a corner and stuck my finger in. I sniffed it. I stuck the finger in my mouth. The powder turned to a sticky glue on my teeth. I re-sealed the tub for later.

Exploring further I found some steel-walled compartments built under the bench seats that lined either side of the cargo hold. I swung a few open and found rusty tools, bundles of wires and containers of bolts and screws. They were for repairing the machine, I guessed.

At the rear of the cargo hold I pulled down a heap of containers to uncover a locked steel compartment larger than the others. It was welded to the floor and had a slanted lid and I'd have probably assumed that it contained the same worthless junk I found scattered everywhere else in that rolling shithole. But this compartment, unlike the others, was locked with a heavy brass padlock. And the lock was shiny from frequent handling and use.

That meant there was something good inside.

I stumbled forward over the heaps of debris to where the two assholes lay dead in their own shit and puke. I held my breath and patted their pockets where I found mostly hard candies. They both had cartridges and shotgun shells in their pockets. I'd look for the guns that went with them later. There was a dead wristwatch with a cracked glass face. A tiny statue of a smiling man seated with legs folded. A small metal box of matches. Even a few ancient coins with faces of men I didn't know engraved on them. I scattered them all to the floor as I searched. I found everything except keys. I pulled open the shirt of the corpse with that stupid striped toque still jammed low on his head. There on a chain around his throat was a shiny key with the same marks stamped on it as the lock had. A silhouette of a bear rearing up on its hind legs.

The key fit the lock and I prized the barrel free of the loops and worked it from the hasp. I was reaching for the pull handle to raise the lid when it exploded upward all on its own. I stumbled back to fall on my ass. The fingers of a gloved hand gripped the lip of the open compartment. I cleared the revolver from the pocket of the yellow parka and sat pointing the barrel at a dark shape rising from the compartment making animal sounds from behind black staring eyes.

T he shape stood in the open compartment looking at me through impossibly huge lidless eyes. It was humped over with arms limp at its sides. Its shoulders rose and fell in rhythm with the hissing and sucking sounds coming from a tank suspended below its mouthless face by a segmented length of plastic hose.

I shouted something and jabbed the revolver forward as the thing's hands rose to its head and, with a jingle of clasps, released the mask from its face and fell forward with a gasp.

The mask, a gas mask, dropped to the metal deck with the thump. The man fell atop it. He lay there with gloved hands clawing, drawing in breaths with loud wet gulps.

Even though he wore a heavily padded coverall over layers of other clothing I could tell the man wasn't much bigger than me. His face was narrow with large bulbous eyes and a weak, quavering chin. His scalp was bare except for a few patches of long thin strands of red hair. His skin was nearly blue from being folded up and nearly asphyxiating in that metal box.

I couldn't talk from pure shock and he couldn't talk because he was having trouble filling his lungs. He lay sipping air through clenched teeth and recovered enough to raise up to a sitting position. I got to my feet and backed away against a heap of containers with the revolver lined up on him. He waved a hand at me feebly.

"It's okay. You know it. It's all right, boy," he said with a croak.

"You were with them," I said.

"I was with them. You know it. But not with them like that," he said and lowered the hand to his lap.

"You rode with them. You were with them. You were their friend."

"I wasn't their friend. You know it. You lock your friends in boxes. You do that to your friends."

"I don't have any friends."

"I am not surprised by that. You know it. That is no surprise to me at all."

"Why are you here if you're not one of them." I said.

"I am here because they know shit-all about keeping the Beast running. You know it. They know shit-all about fuel and batteries and all. You know it."

"The Beast."

"The Beast! The Beast!" He waved a hand around him. "You're in the Beast! You know it. They drive it but I make it go, keep it going."

"And now the Beast is mine," I said, tilting the gun in my hand so he could see it.

He nodded.

"You know it," I said.

He nodded again.

He told me his name was Fingers and he swore he could get the Beast moving again. All he needed to do was go outside and look at the motor. Swore he was a prisoner of the three men I killed. Hard to argue with that since I found him locked inside a box like he said.

Still, I didn't trust him. Unlocking that box and saving his life didn't make us friends. Not turning my back on anyone was bred into my bones. I had to work out how I could use him to get the Beast working and not have him run off on me. Wasn't even sure if he was lying about fixing the Beast. He'd say anything to stay alive a little more. I know I would.

"This is how we're doing this, Fingers," I told him. "You're gonna climb up top. I'll have this gun on you the whole time. You climb down off the machine and call to me so I can tell where you are. You got that."

"Climb out. Yell to you when I'm clear. No funny stuff. You know it," he said, his head bobbled up and down like it was on a spring.

"No funny stuff," I said and jerked the gun at the mouth of the hatch above us.

He kept talking, kept letting me hear him the whole way up and out. None of it made sense to me. His foot thumped on the ladder rungs outside in descending order. I heard him call out finally, his voice coming from a distance.

I climbed up on top and found Fingers standing a good ways out on the ice. He had his hands held clear of his sides. He kept looking from the body of the bare-assed bearded guy to me.

"Back up some more. I'm coming down," I said.

"Moving now. You know it. Backing up. You see me," he said stepping back and nodding the whole way.

He stayed put while I climbed down.

"Show me how you get this thing started," I said and motioned with the gun.

I followed Fingers to the rear of the machine. He clambered up on the treads and unlatched a section of cowling. I clucked my tongue at him and he held his hands clear while I climbed up atop the treads by him. He raised the insulated cowling section and I held the gun on him. I wanted to be sure he didn't have any kind of weapon squirreled away in there.

I looked inside the engine compartment at the big greasy motor mounted in there. It was all a bewilderment of cables, hoses, wires, intakes, manifolds, drums and terminals. There was no way I knew what the hell I was looking at but still it fascinated me. It was silent and dead and looked like so much lifeless metal to me. There were places where condensation had pooled and turned to ice.

"What's wrong with it," I wanted to know.

"Choked out. Fuel line's dry. You know it. Beast needs a drink," Fingers said.

"What's it drink."

"Kero. Diesel. Gasoline. Alkie. You know it. Run on almost anything that burns."

"Get some."

"I got to climb down to get it. You know it."

"Climb down. But stay where I can see you."

He dropped to the snow and unlatched some clasps that held a battered steel can to the side of the machine. There was a whole row of the cans strapped down tight down along the flank of the vehicle. I remembered seeing more down the other side and more lashed onto a platform at the rear. Looked like this Beast got thirsty a lot.

I watched Fingers at work. He stripped off his gloves and worked with bare hands to unclip a flat metal canister from atop the motor and set it aside. That exposed a complicated mechanism that shone with oil and had four throats atop it with levered valves that swung open easy under Finger's touch. He seemed pleased to find them not frozen and swinging free. He uncapped the steel can and poured a tiny measure, just a splash, into each of the throats.

"That's all it takes. Only a few drops," I asked.

"Just a sip to prime it. Don't want to flood it. You know it," he said and recapped the can.

I didn't know it. I didn't know shit. There were a million questions to ask and I didn't know enough even to ask even one. I didn't have the words yet for what I was seeing.

Fingers replaced the flat metal canister and snapped the closures home. Then he hiked himself up to lean deeper into the engine compartment to grip some cables there. I leaned close by him to watch him free the end of one cable, a bundle of shiny bare wiring bristled from the end of it. He touched the bare wires to a terminal at the end of a barrel-shaped deal and there was a spray of sparks and a wisp of blue smoke.

The engine came to life with a deafening roar that scared the shit out of me. I backed away forgetting that I was standing on a slick surface only two feet across. My foot swung in open air and I flailed my hands for any kind of grip. In my panic I let go of the revolver and it went flying from my hand. I hit the crusted drift flat on my back. I had the wind knocked from me. I rolled to the foot of the drift fighting to draw in even a single mouthful of air.

I lay there gasping and looking up at Fingers still standing above me. He was turned away tinkering with something in the engine compartment. The machine throbbed with power making a rumbling growl that rose and fell as Fingers fiddled with something or other. The sound dropped from a roar to a steady purr. Fingers seemed satisfied. He lowered the cowling and clapped the latches closed.

I recovered enough to sit up and look around for where the revolver fell. I was on hands and knees brushing my hands over the snow looking for it when I heard Fingers clucking his tongue above me just like I'd done to him. He was standing on the treads holding the revolver in his hand. It wasn't aimed at me particularly. He was only holding it and smiling down at me. It was a damned peculiar smile. It showed all those horse teeth of his and reached all the way to his eyes.

He took the pistol in both hands and I turned away pressing my eyes closed. Something dropped on me. Then some other somethings pattered onto the hard crust around me. I opened my eyes and looked up.

Fingers had snapped the cylinder of the revolver open and dropped the cartridges down on me. Then he underhand tossed the gun well away before dropping the fuel can to the snow and following after himself.

"Told you I wasn't with them. You know it. Told you those fuckers locked me up like a dog. Fed me shit. You let me out," he said and held out a hand to help me to my feet.

"So. What now," I said.

"You live here. You got people. You know it. Family."

"Yeah. I have people."

"Help me clean up the Beast. I'll share some goodies with you. For your family. You know it."

"Then what."

"I take the Beast. Head back up the Snake. Go back to the Boss. You know what. He'll shit when he sees old Fingers is still alive."

I had no idea what any of that meant except that Fingers had a place to be, a place where he belonged and was anxious to get back to.

"Why help me. I might have shot you," I said.

"You didn't. You know what. You didn't shoot me," he said and showed me those horse teeth again.

And I guess that was enough for him. But not for me. Not by a long shot was it going to be enough for me.

W e hauled the two bodies out and dumped them in the snow
     after I went through their pockets.

Snow was falling hard and had been for hours. A wind was carrying it near sideways and drifting it against the flanks of the big truck. Just as well. Hard weather kept curious eyes away.

I took a sack and filled it with as much canned goods and hard candies as I could find around the inside of the machine. The shotgun was down between the front seats, an old double barrel with a carved wooden stock. The barrels were worn almost smooth but I could still see where there were animals and trees engraved in the metal, prancing deer and hopping rabbits and some kind of animal with broad wings and a long neck. It was well-oiled and broke open easy enough. Fingers said I was welcome to it. There was a coffee can filled with cartridges for it. I took them and all the rest of the shells I could find littered over the floor. Found shells for the revolver too and a bone-handled knife in a tooled leather sleeve. Fingers told me to keep it all to make up for the assholes running over my rifle.

Fingers unbolted a few of the covers from the vents and let cold fresh air in to relieve some of the stink. Then he thawed buckets of snow and washed the puke off the deck plates and let the warm water run out through a cock he pried open in the floor.

"Dumb shits didn't know nothing. Didn't know what Fingers knows. You know what. Locked me up the only place I could breathe while they strangled on diesel," he grinned as he sopped up the last of the water with filthy rags.

It was still coming down wet and white when I helped him lift fuel cans up to the intake where he topped the Beast's tanks off. He opened a compartment recessed in the side of the machine and pulled out a bundle wrapped in oiled cloth bound with wire. Fingers handed it to me. It was heavy and froze solid.

"A caribou haunch. You know what. Feed your people a while. Plenty for Fingers so I want you to have it," he said.

I didn't have the words. My throat swelled up like it was going to choke me and I didn't know what it was. Gratitude was something I never experienced before. It was my first encounter with kindness and it threw me. No one in this world gave. All they did was take.

Fingers just showed me his teeth and crinkled his eyes.

I guess he figured I gave him his life and he was giving back what he could.

I sat in the seat by him while he worked the levers, pedals and the wheel to back the machine off the drift and pilot it through the gap to leave the stadium. The vents at the front were cranked open. I leaned forward to guide him between the heaps of ruins to the warm hole.

"Right or left," he'd say.

I'd look at him and shake my head.

"Don't know right from left. You know what. This is left. This is right," he said and pointed this way and that.

Didn't mean shit to me. I guess my face told him that and he laughed. It was a high giggling laugh like the girl in the yellow parka made but not musical like the sound she made. Not pretty at all.

"Just point. You know what. You just point which way I go," he said and turned the wheel to bring the machine about toward whichever way I pointed.

As we got closer to where the warm hole was hidden I started thinking maybe it was a trick. Maybe Fingers was being kind to find out where my people were. Maybe he wanted to hurt them or rob them. I watched him at the wheel, squinting into the glare coming in through the vents, jamming the levers back and forth as the machine climbed a drift or descended an icy slope. Then I laughed myself. He turned and looked at me, an eyebrow arched.

"Something funny. You know what. Tell me and I'll laugh too," he said smiling.

"Nothing. I don't know why I laughed," I said.

But I did. I was amused at the idea of anyone wanting to rob the old man. Fingers had a wonderful warm machine and more food in one container than my people saw in one place their whole lifetimes. What the hell could he want from the shithole I called home.

We reached the flat area of ice in front of the ruin that hid the warm hole. Fingers geared down and braked and set the machine to idle. I tossed the sack holding the 'bou haunch, candy and tinned food out through the hatch and climbed up after with the shotgun strapped to my shoulder on a sling I made from bundled wires. I made an insulating layer of quilted cloth I'd cut from the back of one of the asshole's coats and bound it with wire around the barrels and forestock. I knotted more cloth around the hammers and action. It would still break open for re-loading but be protected from the cold.

Before I lowered the hatch closed I looked down at Fingers standing on the deck looking up at me with a sad smile.

"You'll be all right. You know what. You're a smart one. You'll be all right," he said.

I had nothing to say to that. I shut the hatch and listened to the grinding squeal of him dogging it closed from inside.

I dropped to the snow, picked up the sack and stepped clear. The Beast backed up away from me. I couldn't see Fingers through the vents but I knew he'd see me. I raised a hand to him then he backed around and, with a jerk, trundled forward through the fresh powder and away. I stood listening to the rumble long after the machine vanished in the fog of falling white.

The snow was banked high over the hidden opening. I unslung the shotgun and used the stock end like a shovel to clear away the drift from the barricade.

Except the barricade wasn't there. The furniture and other junk I'd hauled in place days before was pushed in and scattered.

Someone had come since I'd left. Since the heavy snow. Maybe someone was still inside.

I dug in my pockets for two shotgun shells and held them in my teeth while I thumbed back the twin hammers and raised the barrels up to eye level.

I moved slow and cautious down the levels to the warm hole. My hood was pulled clear of my head so I could listen. The cold followed me in through the entrance. If there was anyone here they'd know I was here when the chilled draught reached them. I crouched as I made my way, step-by-step, down to the lair under the ice. I wished now I'd fired the shotgun at least once as a test. There was no way of knowing if it even worked. I had the revolver loaded and tucked warm against my belly. And there was that long blade with the bone handle resting in the sheath on my hip. If there was someone waiting down there for me I'd see they were sorry for it. Taking a man's life meant nothing to me now. Meant less to me than skinning a rabbit or braining a dog.

I stopped short of the curtain of blankets that covered the opening to the warm hole. I held my breath and listened hard, blinking to bring more light into my eyes like the old man taught me.

There was a tiny scraping and rasping sound. More like hundreds of tiny sounds working all at once with short high-pitched yips and squeals between. I knew the sound. I heard it before lots of time deep in the dark of the lower floors in the buildings we scavenged.

Rats.

And the sound of little teeth working at bone.

The old man's head was busted in. He had no more face. The rats had been at it. The woman who wanted me to call her mother lay with her throat cut, a black spray of blood frozen where she lay face down on her favorite blanket, the one with blue and green flowers on it. Her clothes rustled with the rats working on her underneath.

The kids, my little brother and sister were gone along with anything else that might be of use. The cook pan, the dented steel bowl, the carving knife, and even the shitpot. The old man's and mother's boots were gone. The rats had already chewed away the many layers of socks and gnawed the flesh of their feet down to the yellow joints.

No sign of the kids at all. Someone thought they had enough value not to waste them.

I left the hole to go back up to the surface. The snow had stopped after dumping two feet of fresh white that covered any tracks left by the strangers, or neighbors, who did the old man and his woman. Only one set of tracks was visible in the powder.

The Beast.

I couldn't hear it any more. It was off somewhere the other side of the buildings heading for the Big Ice like Fingers told me he would. I picked up the sack and ran a straight course for the banks that lead down to the ice. The machine would have to pick its way around the ruins and drifts to make its way down. I could cut straight across and meet it where it rolled out on the flat surface.

I climbed hummocks and snow and ran down narrow lanes between the crowns of the buried buildings. I was flying along across places I knew were hunting grounds for animals and humans too. And I ran without caution because that smelly old truck was my magic carpet, my chariot. It was the only way to a life away from this slow death I'd known since the day I was born. Staying was no kind of choice. How long would I last on my own, a kid by himself hiding like one of those rats in the wreckage of a dying place. How many days till I just starved to death. How many nights until some pack of two-legged wolves found me and slit my neck open or worse. How long until I went plain crazy from having no one but me to rely on.

I risked it all on that run to cut off the truck and beg Fingers to take me up the Snake to see the Boss. I didn't even know what it meant but I knew with every beat of my heart that it had to be better than what I was leaving behind.

My lungs were on fire and the stitch in my side felt like a hot clamp under my ribs by the time I reached the high bank that lead down to the table-flat stretch of ice that lay uninterrupted to the horizon and beyond. The Beast was trundling down an embankment far to my left ahead of a cloud of powder raised by the rolling treads. A jet of blue exhaust rose out of the stack as the engine gunned for the open ground. I'd have yelled but I had no breath and Fingers would never hear me anyway.

Sliding and stumbling I made my way down the bank to make the ice. I could still reach him if he turned my way by cutting straight across the curve. I watched him as I ran dead out. The nose of the Beast rotated my way for a course that would pass a few hundred yards in front of me. I ran hard, hugging the sack in my arms, the shotgun banging on my shoulder with each step. My chest hurt like hell with every frigid breath I drew in. My heart worked like a hammer on an anvil. My eyes stung with freezing tears.

I stumbled once, my heel sliding out from under me on the slick surface hiding under the new fall of snow. I tossed aside the sack. I'd need my hands to keep my balance. Arms pumping, I forgot everything but making it to the path that the Beast would cross before me.

As I ran I heard the rumble and felt the tremor through the ice beneath me. The big truck crunched through the freezing crust just before me. I poured on more speed, lifting my boots clear of the powder with head down in a last burst of speed.

The Beast just kept passing further, angling away from me even as I changed my course to follow. I would never catch up. I drew to a stop and unslung the shotgun to fire one and then the other barrel in the air. The Beast kept moving away across the big ice on a course to follow the shoreline rising up to describe where the ocean once met the land.

I dropped to my knees gasping and hugging my aching ribs. My mouth was dry from drawing in freezing air and I forced myself to clamp my jaws shut before my gums and tongue froze solid. I pressed my eyes shut and felt the ice crystals of my own tears grind between the lids.

The sun was falling toward the edge of the ice and I forced myself back to my feet to walk back to where I dropped the sack. I crouched over it and reloaded the shotgun from the cache of cartridges on my pocket.

This was the crossroads. Behind me lay the place I was born, the only place I'd ever known. In front of me was miles and miles of nothing but ice with no shelter from the wind, no way to make a fire, no place to hide if predators of any kind found me.

I slung the shotgun, shouldered the sack and set off to cross the trail of the Beast and follow it to wherever it called home.

Or die out on the ice trying.

WINTERWORLD ❄ CHUCK DIXON

W alk or die.
I followed the tracks through the night and into the dawn light. The wind blew them away in places and I'd pick them up further on.

Fingers was keeping the shoreline to his right, following the line of the land. I only had to keep on steady. I told myself that he had to stop sometime to sleep or piss or take a shit. If I could only keep walking and never stop I'd find him.

Amazing what bullshit you can talk yourself into.

The further I walked away from where I'd come the less real it seemed to me and the less sense it all made. I hunted down those men and killed them for a girl I'd never met and would never even know the name of. I got furious enough to kill three men for her and no regrets. I cried for her. My heart ached for her pain.

Yet I felt nothing for the old man and his woman. I'd spent every day of my life with them and their deaths meant less to me than losing that rifle. And the kids. They were taken from the warm hole to what. Someone thought they were valuable or useful. Valuable for what purpose I'd never know. To what use were they put. And why didn't I try to find who took them. My heart wasn't dead because I felt the loss of the girl in the yellow parka. I felt bad about not feeling bad for what happened to my own family. Who knows the human heart, the mind of a man. I damned sure don't claim to.

I sucked candies as I walked. I swung my arms before me to make heat under the layers of clothes. I stamped my feet on the ice to keep

64

the blood moving. I fought to keep my eyes from closing. My head ached from squinting my eyes against the sun's glare off the frozen caps of crust stretching before me to the end of the earth. I wore my goggles but they weren't enough. Using the knife I cut a strip from the sleeve of the parka and made a slit for my eyes and tied it around my head and placed the goggles over the band. It helped a little but the light still felt like a blade cutting into my skull more and more with every step.

The tracks of the Beast stretched out before me, making a lazy curve around an escarpment that formed a headland I couldn't see over. As the trail got closer to the base of the ice shelf the curve sharpened. It turned in closer to follow the wall of ice columns at the foot of the headland. I trudged on, head down and eyes on the tracks until they moved into the shadow the steeply rising ground cast on the ice with the rising sun.

I looked up when the sun was full overhead shining down through clouds that were dull silver like a fish's belly. It surprised me to see now that there was land on either side of the ice now. The tracks were moving down a channel between white masses of land. From where the sun was I judged that the machine had turned away from the Big Ice and was now angling deeper into the hills of snow. I could see ahead that the channel was narrowing where the hills closed in from either side. The Beast was not in sight but the tracks were still plain to see and sheltered somewhat from the wind by the enclosing banks. It was some comfort that I was no longer walking out into the nothingness of the Big Ice. It felt for the first time like I was heading somewhere.

I had a destination.

T he ice shelves rose higher on either bank as the day wore on to
  night. I could see structures here and there. Smoke smeared
across the sky from fires I couldn't see. That put some heat on my ass
to keep moving. No problem at all picking out a solitary shape and
my bright yellow parka in all that white. Anyone up on the shores
would have their eyes and ears open as the machine passed this way
only a few hours before me.

Toward dusk I hunkered down low to let a pack of wolves pass. They
were a half mile ahead and moving single file. A big pack. I lost count
after twenty. I was only glad I was downwind from them.

A sideways squall picked up as full dark came on. It was chipping
the peaks off the crust like a million invisible blades. The tracks left by
the Beast were being swept over. I was dizzy with exhaustion. My legs
felt like sacks of lead. My arms were too heavy to raise. Still, I leaned
into the wind and picked it up to a trot to keep to the trail while it was
still plainly visible. I could follow the river of ice and still lose the Beast
if it turned off and up one of the banks. It would be the easiest mistake
to just keep on keeping on past where Fingers left the ice for home.

A ridge of icy escarpment jutted out ahead. The wide ice path turned
away out of sight behind it. I kept moving, feet shuffling and head down
looking for any sign of wheel tracks. A sharp scent on the wind brought
me to a halt. An oily smell drifted to me over the ice. The taste on the
back of my tongue told me it was diesel fumes. I was close enough to
the machine to smell it.

I dug down deep for the last bit of energy I had and broke into a near run to reach the other side of the finger of high ice. As I rounded it I saw, a mile or so ahead, where the span of a bridge started on the far bank. More and more of the bridge came into view as I ran. There was a growing bitterness in the cloud of diesel stink blowing toward me. I could see a gray haze swirling low atop the ice. It thickened to hide the details of the bridge from me.

When I cleared the point of the promontory I could see the full length of the bridge and the source of the smoke cloud. A fire glowed beneath the bridge near center span. It was a lake of burning fuel. In the middle of it the Beast sat unmoving.

In the shifting glow of the fire I could see a figure hanging from beneath the bridge.

I knew even before I got close enough to see that it was Fingers.

The corpse was strung up by the ankles to slow roast over the blaze. His clothes had been cut away. His skin shriveled to his bones, crisped brown. Fat dripped from the ends of his charred hair. He could have been anyone, only I recognized those horse teeth of his. The heat had shrunk his lips away to make a kind of cartoon of his smile. He swung slowly back and forth in the heat, a wire around his ankles was suspended from a crossbeam somewhere along the bridge's understructure.

The fire was dying, the fuel boiling away. The black cloud of poisonous smoke was being torn away by the high wind toward the far bank. I was able to get close enough to find where the wire that hoisted Fingers up was secured to a bolt on a bridge upright. With the knife he gifted me I sawed until the last stand of cable parted. Fingers dropped into the fire landing somewhere out of my sight on top of the Beast. He struck with a damp thump. It was a rotten resting place but a damned sight better than swinging where all the world could see his naked broiled ass.

Like any kindness, this one had its own retribution. It came on fast.

Black shadows up under the bridge started moving and coming apart in the dying firelight. Men who looked like piles of rags with minds of their own were sliding down support angles and dropping to lower beams. They were calling and hooting. Something landed in the melted slush near me, splashing me. A hammer with a broad head. More shit started raining down as the ragmen dropped closer and closer.

I raised the shotgun. One barrel followed by the other. They were wild shots. I didn't stay to see the damage. I turned and ran back the way I came, cutting through the thick curtain of black smoke. The sack was forgotten behind me. I tried re-loading the shotgun on the run. My hands shook so that I kept dropping shells. The hoots rose high, close behind me. I threw the shotgun aside. My legs pumping, I dug for the revolver. I thumbed the hammer back.

I'd taken these assholes' dinner and I'd be the one to replace it.

The calls ranged out behind. They were keeping track of one another in the blinding smoke cloud. When I broke through the fog into the clear I looked back once. There were more than I could count and they'd spread out with their fastest runners looking to draw even with me on either side. I fired off a snap shot as I ran. It didn't slow them a half step even. I pumped legs and arms and ran flat out. My lungs burned. My chest hammered. My brain felt like a trapped animal squirming behind my eyes. Is this the way out. This. This.

I was tired beyond tired, way past my best and coming up on not caring if they caught me or not so long as I could rest a moment. There was everywhere to run but not one place to hide. They were going to catch up or ring me in. It was a matter of time, a matter of the next few steps.

There was a high whine that reached me. Nothing an animal would make but a mechanical noise. Off to my left a shape was tearing over the ice in a broad loop toward the direction I was running. It turned sharp and crossed my path maybe fifty paces in front of me to come to a full stop. It was a figure in a full face mask under a black helmet and wearing a long canvas coat. The figure was straddling a machine with skis in front and a pair of treads in the back. I was cut off with the machine and rider in my path. I stopped to raise my revolver in a last act of defiance.

The rider had already pulled a short rifle from a kind of boot mounted on the machine and was working a lever and firing from the hip.

Something moved close past my ear with a crackling sound as it whipped by. I turned to see one of the ragmen leave the ice, his foot kicked out to send up a spray of snow. A second ragman folded to go sliding on the ice. A third spun backwards and a fourth just kind of jerked to a sudden stop before falling to his knees. The rest of them slid to a halt. They stared dumbly at the slaughter before them. One of the fallen flopped on the ice gurgling. It couldn't have taken much more than a heartbeat.

I turned back to the rider who was waving a mittened hand to me.

I ran to the machine and jumped on the back. The engine shrieked and throbbed under me. Together we shot out over the ice.

W e didn't drive directly away from the ragmen like I dearly wished we would.

The rider turned the machine hard enough to lift one ski from the ice. I locked my fists behind me on a steel grip bar I found there. I shoved the revolver in a pocket to use that hand to hold on. My boot kicked up a furrow of snow at the steepest part of the curve. The rider straightened the bars and we sailed back toward the bridge. I'd never moved so fast in my life, the cold air turning my face numb as we cut through it. I reminded myself to breathe.

Black figures lined the top of the span to throw stuff down on us as we got closer. I saw steel bars, rods, stones and bricks striking all around us. The rider swerved around a bucket loaded with gravel that exploded right in front of us. We roared under a section of the span with the ceiling so low above us I ducked lower in my seat.

Coming out the other side there was nothing but wide open white except for the burned humps of other wrecks covered over with drifts. I guessed these were other victims of the ragmen. I almost crossed under that bridge on foot. I'd have been dead in two steps and hung up to roast in three.

The ski machine was loud enough to hurt my ears. There was no way to talk to the rider. At that point I knew enough about them, right. They pulled my ass out of a bad situation. I could have wound up swinging from my heels like poor Fingers.

Of course, I've hunted enough to see one predator take another's meal. I was safe for now but there was no guarantee this was a rescue.

I could have been taken from the ragmen just to fill someone else's belly. Or to fill some other need that I didn't want to think about right then. But for the moment, and for who knew how many more moments, I was safe.

Together we skimmed over the crust with the rider having to adjust to the biting wind ripping down over the ice off the far bank. We stayed center of the stream with open ice to either side. Along the banks I saw the ruins of what were once tall buildings. The hulks of boats sat along one shoreline crushed under the weight of their own rot and rust. They were canted in their berths with snow banked high along their hulls and snarls of masts and lines joining them one to another in impossible tangles. Lights winked from portholes as we passed by. A grimy smear rose from a tilted smokestack. This river of ice was home to more than just the ragmen.

We left the corroded jumble of boats and the dead city behind. It hit me all at once how tired I was. My hands ached where they gripped the smooth steel rod behind me. My eyes were getting heavy, my sight was fuzzy around the edges. Rising warmth off the throbbing engine below radiated through my layers of clothing. I let go of the rod and leaned against the back of the rider. The rider took one of my wrists and then the other and pulled my arms like a belt around his waist. I joined my hands over his belly and that's the last I remembered for a while.

I came back around when I felt a hand grip my wrist hard. We were moving up a steep incline, a kind of channel lined with slanted concrete walls either side. I took my hands from the rider's waist to put them back on the rail behind me, leaning my weight back to match the rise of the front end of the machine as it climbed.

We came level again and the machine slowed from a high whine to a rumbling purr. There were openings on either side of the channel. Some had a lattice of thick iron bars before them. Others were choked closed with heaps of debris. The rider shut the engine down and the machine glided to a halt. I climbed off behind the rider who took the bars of the machine to push. I put my hands to the rear cowling and pushed as well. I didn't say anything, kept my questions to myself. We were rolling quiet for a reason. My eyes swept those dark openings. Nothing moved there. That didn't mean a thing. There could be a hundred eyes on us looking for an opening. I dug in and pushed harder.

The rider stepped from the bars and I dropped to the ice, the machine skating to a stop. We'd come to one of the barred openings. It was different from the others. It didn't have piles of ice-rimed rubbish in front of it. The rider moved to the bars and I saw there was a gate built into the center of it with heavy chains wrapped tight around one side of the frame. The chain was cinched closed by a big steel lock covered with a coat of clear ice. The rider took a hatchet off his belt and used the mallet end to hammer the ice off the chain and lock then stuck a key in the lock and freed the chain. I helped kick new snow away from the gate and we both pulled it open with a rasping squeak from the hinges. We then pushed the ski machine inside. The opening was the end of a wide corridor with a curved ceiling of chipped concrete. Once the machine was well out of sight down the dark tunnel the rider went back and re-secured the chain and lock with the lock on the inside now.

Coming back, the rider pulled down the hood and face mask. She shook her head to free a long mane of light brown hair and looked at me with eyes the color of the green on mother's favorite blanket.

She smiled crooked at the face I was probably making.

"Never seen a girl before," she said.

"Sure. Yah. I've seen girls before," I said feeling stupid but I wasn't sure why. She was a girl, I guess. Older than me by a few years. Younger than my mother by a lot more. I realized that, without the helmet, she was the same height as me.

"You cut that man down back there. What was he to you," she said.

"I helped him. He gave me some food. I thought I'd follow him and see where the Beast was going."

"The Beast," she said and nodded. "So, you did know Fingers. And you are alone. You're alone, right."

"Yah. That's why I was following him."

"You have a name," she said.

"Yes," I answered, but wouldn't say the name the old man called me. She laughed again.

"Well, Mister Yes, my name is Cilla. Let's go meet the Boss."

W e walked a long ways down that tunnel into a bunch of big dark rooms. Cilla kept talking but I can't remember much of what she said. I was too busy looking around. The rooms we walked through were huge with ceilings so high I couldn't see them. There were shafts of weak light coming down from above as though shining through water. The floors were cracked concrete the same as the walls and here and there were steel uprights covered over in thick orange rust. I could still see my breath in front of me but it felt warmer here. Maybe because we were out of the wind.

The ceiling dropped as we came to a long corridor that was wide enough side to side for twenty or more people to walk with arms held full out at their sides. At the end of it was a glow getting bigger and brighter as we walked closer. A smell reached me of cooking food and machine oil. The air was rich with it by the time we exited into a large area dimly lit with some kind of bulbs spaced wide all around the walls.

There was a pool of brighter light cast down from a hanging array. One wall was lined with a work bench and that wall was hung with rows of tools of all kinds, all shining with a sheen of oil and free of rust. The long bench had machines mounted on it and more machines were free-standing on the concrete floor. It was warmed by a drum-shaped stove with a long pipe stuck from one end to run up to a vent opening high on the wall. A stock pot bubbled and popped on top of the drum, leaking a steam that made my stomach clench like a fist. My mouth watered.

Of all these wonders the one that stopped me in my tracks was a big machine, the biggest I'd ever seen, squatting in the center of the open space. It sat up high on four triangular treads twice as tall as me and wider across than I could spread my arms from fingertip to fingertip. Up on those mighty treads and atop thick steel legs bent like an animal set to spring was a long cabin of angled armor-steel plate and a vented engine housing. Big block letters long faded and scratched read: CAT along the side of one plate. If Fingers' machine was the Beast then this was its mother. There were ladders and scaffolding around it and places where hatches or cowling had been removed. I may not have known jack shit about mechanics back then but even I could see that this was a work in progress.

Cilla was talking again but not to me.

There was someone seated at that workbench. I hadn't seen him before because of the bad light and the high backed chair he was sitting in. The figure stood now, raising up in a careful motion that let me know he was either crippled or old. The man was surprisingly tall, the biggest man I'd ever seen even though he was stooped with a bent back. He had a thick woolen cap pulled down to his thick white eyebrows. A long white beard and broad mustache covered everything below his cheeks. He moved closer taking careful steps, taking his time because he had to. I had to look up to meet his eyes.

This was the Boss. No one needed to tell me that.

"Can you read," he said. His voice was a low rumble like thunder heard through thick snow clouds.

"Some. If there's pictures," I said.

"Then he's not a complete idiot," he said to Cilla. He emphasized the word complete.

"Let's see your hands," he said to me.

I looked at him, not understanding.

"Get those mittens and gloves off, boy. Show me your hands," he said, insistent but not mean.

I pulled off the mittens and two pairs of rough cloth gloves until my hands and fingers were bare.

He reached out with his own hands to take mine. His fingers were bony rigid claws, the joints swollen and locked in a permanent grasp. They were warm on mine but with little strength in them as he brought a gentle pressure to my palm and wrists. He brushed the callouses of my fingers with his own rougher skin.

"Small but strong. And they're rough with all the digits in place. The boy's not afraid to work," the Boss said and the corners of his eyes crinkled to let me know he was smiling.

"I'll work," I said.

Shit, I didn't know what work meant. I mean real work not just digging in the slush for a can of beans or a scrap of wood to burn.

"That's good. That's fine. That's real fine," he said and let go my hands to turn to Cilla who was studying me hard with those deep green eyes.

"So, he's gonna be your new Fingers," she said.

I n this life you have to take what you can but you can never keep it. You might find it. You might even have it given to you. But one thing is for damn sure, nothing is yours forever.

Those days, working with the Boss, might not have been happiness. What the hell is that. But it was sure different from what I came from.

I had a full belly most days. I was warmer than I'd ever been. I worked my ass off, sure. The Boss drove me hard. Only he was never mean. He never hit me or even said an unkind word meant to wound. For a big man he had no idea of his bigness. Even crippled up as much as he was, he could have kicked my ass any time he wanted. It never crossed his mind. He wasn't built that way. Whatever hurt he had he didn't make anyone share it with him.

Most important to me was I had a reason to get up in the morning for something besides looking for food or because the old man would have busted me one for sleeping too long.

I called the underground place the Garage because that's what the Boss called it and that's what it was. It was a goddamned miracle, a piece of the old, forgotten world still functioning and moving ahead all on its own.

The Boss needed me to act as his hands to work the tools to get that big monster machine built and moving. He called it Leviathan, a name he got from the big hardcover bible he read whenever he wasn't working. I'm not even sure why he read it so much. The Boss could recite so much of it that it seemed like every word of it was up there in his head already.

To use the tools, the presses, the drills, the lathes and welding torches, I had to be taught what they were and how they worked. The

Boss showed me all that and gave me manuals to study and schooled me on reading so I could understand them. It was hard and the days were long and sometimes I thought my skull would bust wide open with all the stuff he was trying to cram in there. But I took to it eagerly and asked questions. I didn't want to be just his Fingers. I wanted to know what he knew. I wanted to know what every tool and every wire, plug, lead and terminal did and why. I didn't want to just have the knowledge of them. I wanted them to be as much a part of me as my arms and legs, toes and fingers.

And when we weren't working to build that big engine up I'd listen to him talk about all kinds of things like how the Earth was made and how man came to rule the world then lose it all. About God's promise to bring the ice next time if man failed to live as he should.

It all made sense to me. It filled in the spaces in my head that used to be filled with questions and no answers. Whatever the hell caused this world to go from a paradise of open water and green hills to being a big ball of dirty ice was a judgment of some kind. You didn't have to be a genius to realize that this was not The Way It Should Be. Men weren't meant to be scratching in the ice for scraps. That was for animals. It stood to reason that if that's what we were brought down to then it was our own fault we fell this far.

We all have an idea of what might have happened. Those are all guesses with no answers. Only a fool, and we meet plenty of them, thinks he knows why winter never ends, why the snow and ice stay with us and the sun brings light but no heat. But knowing that there was a reason, even if none of us knew what it was, brought some comfort even if it was a cold breed of solace.

I spent every day with the Boss while he showed me the purpose of every tool in his shop and schooled me on how they were used until I was able to weld seams and machine all but the finest parts on my own with the help of his library of manuals. Things like springs and levers

I'd need him over my shoulder directing me close. When I made a mistake and spoiled a whole day's work he'd only sigh and say that tomorrow was another day. I'd promise to do better and bust my ass to make that promise true. He'd tell me that mistakes were part of learning too.

Cilla was hardly around. Sure, she lived with us but it was separate.

The only time she spoke to me was to tell me to burn my clothes and take a bath.

"You're a walking lice colony and you stink," she said.

"My blood would freeze," I said.

"It's warm down by the still. There's a tub and hot water and soap," she said.

"I never took a bath in my life," I said.

"Maybe you want me to help you," she said.

My face got hot all of a sudden and she threw back her head and laughed as she walked away. It was a laugh like the girl in the yellow parka but made more in her throat. Not musical but richer.

There was a steel cargo container she lived in and no one was welcome inside there. A fat brass lock made sure of that. She'd eat with us most days but there was little talk between us. I don't know who she was to the Boss. I figured she was just someone he found like me and Fingers. He needed people to do for him and in exchange offered a place that was secure and warm.

Most days, she was gone on her ski machine or would climb up to the surface to scavenge for things we needed. The furthest she traveled from the Garage was the day she went looking for Fingers and found me. Fingers was on a trip out to find tool steel when he run into those three bastards I sent to Hell. Now Cilla took on the scavenging chores all on her own. She never worked on the Leviathan, never picked up a tool or went up the scaffold like Fingers would.

Once in a while the Boss would send me along with her. He said I needed to get out in the sunlight once in a while if I didn't want to stay a shrimp. I didn't know what a shrimp was except that it didn't sound like anything anyone wanted to be. I could always tell that Cilla didn't want to take me along but she never said so.

We'd climb up concrete steps flight after flight until we reached a vertical pipe with a steel ladder set in it. We'd climb this up to a tunnel covered over with grates that let the light in through the snow piled over them. There were steps up from the tunnel that led into a gully lined with stunted evergreen trees kept from growing over the walls of the ravine by the cutting wind. Following this a ways brought us to a wall of brick-covered block with a crack in it just wide enough to let us through one at a time.

Cilla called the place Sam's. I guess because so many things had that name printed on them. The place was an enormous space that had been covered over with snow and ice for so long that I guess everyone forgot it was here. Part of the roof had collapsed in with the weight of the drifts on top of it. There were rows of high steel shelves. Some were still standing upright. Others had fallen against one another collapsing whole rows that spilled their goods into heaps that could only be reached by crawling through the tangles of the steel frames, holding battery-powered lanterns to light our way.

It looked to me like there was more here than anyone would ever need. Sacks of rice, gallon cans of oil, tins of fish and vegetables and fruit. Animals had been at some of it but there was plenty left. Buckets of candy as big as my head. Bags of nuts, bottles of honey and rows of glass and plastic bottles that had burst years before when the cold reached inside them to expand the contents. There were books and paper and all kinds. Then there were sections that made no sense at all. Row after row of shelves with machines of plastic and glass stacked on them and an aisle lined with shelves packed with plastic sleeves that held silver discs as wide across as my hand. On the sleeves were fading pictures of people who always looked either way too happy or way too angry.

There was a heap of goods in one corner where shelves had collapsed. Cilla said these were soaps and medicines and warned me to be careful.

"This stuff's not for eating," she said.

"Then what's it for," I said. I was holding a plastic bottle filled with little white tablets.

"You have to read the labels," she said.

I found boxes that held tubes with the caps exploded off them when the stuff inside exploded.

"What's this," I said.

"Look at the box," she said.

There was a pretty girl on the box holding some kind of stick with a brushy end to her mouth. Her teeth gleamed like new snow.

"You put this on your teeth, right. Why," I said.

"You clean your teeth with it. Look around, there's brushes somewhere," she said.

"I've never done that," I said.

"I know," she said and wrinkled her nose.

There were clothes too. They were all peculiar in that they had legs or sleeves that were too short to cover anyone's arms or legs. I found a stack of shirts of light cloth with short sleeves and big letters on the front spelling USA #1. I picked one out that was big enough to fit over my sweater under my yellow parka. It was light and stretchy and I pulled it over my head. Cilla rolled her eyes when she saw it but didn't say anything.

I found bags of socks and stuffed a few of them in a sack. I'd never had new socks or even clean socks. I wanted to stay longer and explore the whole place but Cilla said we had to go. She'd been here hundreds of times and was bored with the place. To her these runs were just another chore. To me, at first anyway, they were like a journey to another world, a place of mystery and wonder.

We packed two big sacks each and made our way to the gap in the rear wall and down the gully back to the Garage.

I complained that I hadn't seen everything at Sam's. Cilla said there'd be other times.

Me and the Boss talked some times of the day the Leviathan would be finished. Whenever I brought this up he'd start by telling me not to be in a hurry. The work would take a long time and there was no benefit to rushing it. This machine had to be made strong and reliable to survive the trip it was being built for.

The trip to Mechanicsburg.

The Boss heard of the place when he wasn't much older than me. It was a place where men hadn't given over to becoming beasts. It was the Promised Land right out of the book he read all the time. It wasn't a place of milk and honey but it was a place where men still used their brains and their hands to do more than just fill their bellies. The way he described it made it sound like the places in the old magazines I'd seen pictures of. Clean buildings that were warm inside. Lights everywhere so the place wasn't dark all the time. And people could walk where they wanted to and feel safe within the walls of Mechanicsburg.

And most of all it was a place where the old ways weren't forgotten. Men worked together to solve problems. They didn't only think of today but of all the days to come. They were building a place, looking toward the days to come with something other than dull dread. There was no way they could change the world back to what it was but there was sure a way ahead that didn't mean hiding in dark holes with freezing, murder or starvation as the only future to look forward to.

I was just a dumb kid who lived most of his life up to then like a rat in a burrow. Still, I knew a load of shit when I heard it. Mechanicsburg was a story for little kids or a fantasy for a tired old man. Nothing about it made sense. The Boss wasn't even sure where it was. He only sus-pected it was further inland, deeper into the high ice where the Snake led. The Snake, I'd found out, is what he called the river of ice I'd fol-lowed from the Big Ice.

None of it mattered to me. Let him have his Promised Land if that's what he needed to get up out of his bedroll every day. It only mattered to me that I had the Leviathan to work on. To be honest, I'm not sure if I ever cared whether we finished it or not. I was content to live my days in the Garage working on the big machine. I suspect the Boss felt the same way and that Mechanicsburg was a story he told me only to convince himself there was a reason for what we were doing. If both of us told the truth we'd probably say that we didn't care if we ever left this place.

And that day of leaving seemed to be so far in the future. There was so much work to do the way the Boss had it laid out. The mammoth 16-cylinder engine needed a lot of work, including over two hundred missing or worn parts that needed to be tooled from raw metal. On that list was two new rods and pistons to fit into a cylinder bore wide enough for me to put my open hand in and my thumb and little finger could still not touch the opposite walls at the same time. And Cilla was coming up empty on her longer and longer runs to find the quality of metal we needed. In addition to that, the work went so slowly that a lot of our time was taken up on routine maintenance. Bearings and seals would wear out on the supports the body rested on. After doing two rounds of replacement work I convinced the Boss that we needed to remove the huge treads and lower the body of the Leviathan onto a rack so that the weight of thing wasn't undoing our maintenance work all the time. That way we could spend more time building and less time on catch-up.

To accomplish that I found a truck engine that had been discarded among the mountain of scrap that the Boss had collected over time. I rebuilt the engine on my own and got it working to use as the motor for a power winch. The Boss directed me on the construction of a rack that I welded together from steel beams I found discarded at the far end of a tunnel off the Garage. I unbolted the treads from the lift arms and, using the new winch, lowered the body of the Leviathan down on the stout work rack. Cilla reluctantly brought her ski machine from the end of the exit tunnel. We used it to haul the four big triangular tread assemblies clear. I oiled and greased them down and covered them with tarps to keep the frost off the metal. They'd be ready to mount back on the body once the engine was built. And all without the constant maintenance that was stealing so much time from the main work.

Another big advantage of this was we wouldn't have to climb up the scaffolding to work on the engine. We could haul it clean out of the housing on chains using my winch and stand on platforms I welded to the support rack. This would be a lot easier on the Boss's legs and would allow us full access to the power plant without crawling around in the engine compartment.

Yeah, it took a long time. But what's time.

We were resting after accomplishing all that. The Boss said we needed a day off because even God rested after he made the Earth, right.

Cilla was gone on a long run. We threw some extra fuel in the stove. I brought back some books from Sam's. Big thick ones with some woman on the cover smiling with bright eyes. They made for a good fire and the Boss and I sat resting on truck seats enjoying the heat.

I had my first drink on that day.

The Boss got out a bottle made of thick brown glass with a black label. He tore off the paper cover and unscrewed the metal cap.

"Why didn't the glass break. I never seen a bottle that wasn't broke unless it was empty," I said.

"Stuff in here doesn't freeze. Never freezes and never goes bad," he said and poured some into one cup for him and one for me.

"Never goes bad. How's that happen."

"Not only never goes bad, Fingers. It only gets better as time passes."

I was anxious to try anything that only promised to get better, not worse as time went on. I took a long swallow, choked and spat up the whole burning mess while the Boss laughed until all that came out was a whistling wheeze.

"Take it slower, dumbass," he said and poured me a fresh cup.

I sipped it this time and liquid fire trickled into my chest and gut. I sipped some more. Then some more until the knots in my shoulders seem to unwind all on their own and my head felt like it was floating off my shoulders on a string. I started to giggle but had no idea what was so funny.

The Boss had a couple of cups full and was rocking and humming in his chair. It was a tune I'd heard him hum sometimes as we worked. Now he broke from humming to sing the words softly at first and then growing in volume.

> *Life is like a mountain railway*
> *With an engineer that's brave*
> *We must make this run successful*
> *From the cradle to the grave*
> *Heed the curves and watch the tunnels*
> *Never falter, never fail*
> *Keep your hands upon the throttle*
> *And your eye upon the rail*
> *Blessed Savior there to guide us*
> *Till we reach that blissful shore*
> *And the angels there to join us*
> *In God's grace forevermore*

There was more about crossing Jordan and reaching the station. He finished low and drained his cup.

"Is that from the Bible," I said.

"No. It's not," he said and smiled a sad smile and was quiet for a while.

"You're growing, boy. Growing in mind and body," the Boss said. I thought he'd fallen asleep. Or maybe I had.

I just looked at him, head bobbing on that string.

"I see hairs growing on your face. You're even starting to sound like a man when you talk. Walking and standing like a man. The way you rigged that winch, that's man's work. You're a mechanic through and through and fully a man, son."

My head was foggy and my eyes goggling to stay focused but I still caught that he'd called me son. And not in a way that was to make me feel small. He called me that and I felt ten feet tall and ready to take on a pack of wolves with my bare hands.

"Growing out of those old rags too. They're not fit for a mechanic," he said. "You need to wear clothes suited to who you are. Clothes a man would wear."

I sat sipping from my cup while the Boss levered himself up out of his chair with a grunt and made his way back to the workbench where he rooted around in a box there.

He came back with a something of folded blue cloth, dark blue. He handed it to me and I stood up, head light, and let it fall open in my hands. It was a quilted coverall with a zipper front and still had creases from being folded flat for years and years. Unfolded, it was as tall as me and I had to hold it up over my head so the bottom of the legs didn't brush the greasy floor.

"Put it on. It's yours. You earned it," he said.

In the warmth of the fire I stripped down to all but my ragged tighties and that USA shirt that had come to fit me closer since the day I took it from the table at Sam's. I slid my legs in the coverall then my arms into the sleeves and zipped it closed. It fit loose and I had to fold the legs and cuffs up a few courses but it felt fine on me. The Boss motioned me over and cinched up the belt in the back to make it fit a little snugger. It hung just right on my shoulders and the fabric was smooth under my hands. I touched a white disc on my right breast. It was a pad of stiffer cloth sewn there. Inside the oblong a word was stitched in raised red threads.

"What's this," I said.

"The name of the man who once wore that," the Boss said.

"Was he a mechanic too," I said.

"He sure was. He earned that outfit the same way you did," the Boss said.

"Then I want you to call me by his name. I earned his outfit then I earned his name," I said.

"If that's what you want," the Boss said.

My fingers traced the swirling letters of red thread from first letter to last.

Scully.

T he work was going faster now. We were spending all our time
on machining parts for the build. I was skilled enough by now
to do even the smaller, finer parts myself. That left the Boss to cook
up fuel.

The only breaks from the build were runs to Sam's with Cilla. I even
went on a few hunts with her. Once she let me use her rifle, her beloved
Winchester, to bring down a caribou.

The Leviathan was built to accept all kinds of fuel. Anything petro-
based plus alcohol. The Boss had been running a distillery for years. He
stockpiled barrels of engine-grade alkie. The alkie was made from whatever the Boss could find that would ferment or rot. That meant it was
mostly distilled from our own shit and piss. That along with the carcasses
of whatever animals Cilla brought back from her hunts. The Boss found
a nest of baby rats once and they went into the mash. We collected a
mess of those burst bottles at Sam's and they went into the mash too.

The still was kept at the ass-end of a long tunnel under a ceiling of
opened vents to carry the stink away. The mash was kept in a big covered tank. He explained to me that the tunnels and work room were
once part of a water treatment plant for the city that lay in ruins further
down the Snake. People would empty their bowels and flush it away
through miles of pipes. The water would be cleaned and filtered and
turned back into water to drink before being dumped in the river again.
We were doing the same thing only our shit was being turned into fuel.
When the Boss had it going hard it produced a barrel a week.

It was pure poison and he warned me again and again not to drink any of it. He had no worries there.

Anyway, after getting floor-crawling, head-banging, stomach-emptying drunk that first time I had no real desire to try it again anytime soon. Besides, Sam's had stacks of the good stuff if I ever had the urge. Whoever Jack Daniels was he was a very popular guy back before the freeze.

It was looking like it could be done. The transmission and engine would be finished and functioning. The Leviathan would live and carry us all away to Mechanicsburg.

The only hold-up was the pistons and rods for two of the sixteen cylinders. We just didn't have the raw tool steel to fabricate them. The Boss and I pressed Cilla to look for the material we needed or even find a yard or shop with a wreck once powered by a motor like the Leviathan's. Back before his hands and joints locked up on him, the Boss started building the power plant and trannie from a half dozen wrecks he found buried under the ice in a construction yard. They were big machines that he told me they used for making highways and moving mountains. He had a crew then and they spent months breaking the motors down to parts and hauling them back to the Garage. A lot of them were lost along the way and, unless he was into the Jack, he didn't talk about those days. Even then he didn't give many details.

None of us talked about where we came from and what we had to do to get where we were. It's still that way, right. I'm talking now, telling my story. It's not easy, I tell you. Not easy at all.

Cilla mostly did what she wanted to do. She never took it well when we'd press her to look for certain things.

"I provide for you and all you do is bitch," she said all the time. "A crippled up old man and his idiot tool jerk! Who feeds you. Who goes out there on the Snake with all the wasters and wolves. I might just take off on my machine someday and leave you all here to play with yourselves."

Or words to that effect.

She'd either jump on her ski machine and leave us or go to her container and lock herself in.

I waited for a Sam's run to talk to her. I wanted her away from the Boss in case it got ugly. Cilla could call me whatever she wanted and she always did. I just didn't want her being mean to the Boss. He never let on but I knew her words hurt him. He knew he was crippled and wouldn't last many days without us. No need to remind him of that all the time.

And I told her all this when we were picking over cans of chili, looking for ones that wouldn't make us sick. You know, the ones that aren't bloated or pitted with rust spots.

"I do enough," she said.

"All's we need is some raw tool stock," I said.

"Then what," she said.

"We all leave here and go to Mechanisburg."

"That's all shit, total shit, Fingers," she said smirking. She never called me Scully no matter how many times I reminded her.

"It's not. And even if it is, the old man believes in it. It keeps him going and that keeps us going," I said.

"You know what keeps me going," she said and held up a can of chili in my face.

I knocked it from her hand. She screamed at me.

"You think I'm here for you and that cripple. I'm here for all this shit. All the shit you see around you. There's enough for a lifetime and we're the only ones who know it's here. And we're going to leave here to go out there and look for a place that's not going to be there even if we can find it," she screamed in my face, hands fisted and shaking at her sides.

She shoved me back on the pile of chili cans, picked up the lantern and left me to find my way back through the pitch dark.

C illa was gone for days after that. A lot of days.
I thought maybe she made good on her promise to leave us. Or more likely she found another hide nearby. She'd never leave Sam's.

The Boss worried hard that something happened to her outside. Even though Cilla called him names and treated him the way she did, he cared about her enough to keep asking me where she was. I didn't tell him what happened in Sam's, what she said and how she left me there to take the longest time to feel my way out of the maze. I just told him she was delayed or took a long way around. I reminded him how careful she was not to lead wasters back to the Garage. He'd take to his bed with a bottle or spend a lot of time back at his still just sitting alone in the dark.

Cilla came back finally. She didn't say where she'd been or what held her up. She'd hauled back a caribou carcass and I helped her pull it into the Garage to hang. The Boss only grunted a greeting at her, never giving away how torn up he'd been while she was gone who knew where.

It was later, when the Boss had gone to tend the still, that she talked to me. Cilla told me she went a whole day up the Snake and found a collection of ruins. No people lived there. It was all rusting machinery and big stacks of metal plates in a big building filled with junk she couldn't figure out. She'd have brought some of it back but the sheets were too heavy for her to move on her own and there was no way to haul them back with her ski machine.

"I need you to go with me to see if it's what you and the old guy are looking for," she said.

"Yah," I said.

"Can you bang up some kind of sled. Something to haul the stuff back in," she said.

"I can do that," I said.

I told the Boss what we were doing. Cilla told us more about the place she found the metal sheets, describing them and showing us with her hands how thick and how wide the plates were. She said there were rods of steel stacked in bins. The Boss and I decided that I might need to bring the welding tanks and torch with me in case I needed to cut sections to make them easier to haul.

The Boss drew a picture of what the sled might look like to bear up under the load. As twisted as his hands were he could still make these accurate drawings with one of the flat lead pencils he had. Using the drawing I cut the steel pipes and welded a kind of ski trailer together. Then I welded a tow hitch to the back of the ski machine like I saw in one of the Boss's books. It would hold the weight of four people or more. Plenty for the amount of tool metal we needed to finish the build.

We took extra cans of fuel and a spare torch and tanks. I'd leave them behind at the site. The Boss walked us out to where the ski machine was. He said he wanted to check the sled and the tow hitch one last time. He didn't say any more as he we pushed the machine out through the gate. I looked back to see him turning away.

"He's going to be alone," I said.

"We'll be back," she said.

"He's thinking about Fingers. About how he never came back," I said.

"If that happens I'll bring him a new Fingers, Fingers," she said and laughed back in her throat.

I rode back in the sled and she stomped the starter and we were off down the concrete canyon of the Snake.

We would be back. But it wouldn't be the same from then on. For any of us.

T he ski machine was noisy as hell. The high-revving engine
   sound carried for miles. Sounds on the Snake were tricky. The
whine of the racing engine travelled over the ice and bounced back
off the banks easing and falling as it approached and departed. It
was hard to tell where the source was. And it scared more wasters
than it attracted.

We travelled through the long night going full out. We came across
a few bridges. Either we raced under the span or found a way around
if the clearance was too low. Cilla had been this way and knew which
bridges were snares and which were just lonely wrecks. The bridges
usually sat where the ruins were clustered the most. The bridges once
joined two sides of a river with roads leading off in either direction for
days and days to more people and cities. Now they were traps to be
avoided, chokepoints where wasters gathered.

There were boats stuck on the Snake sometimes. Big flat barges,
some mostly submerged in the ice and others sitting on the surface like
a giant hand placed them there. Some of these had smoke columns rising from them. We saw men by a barge fishing in a hole they'd broken
in the ice. We made a wide sweep around them.

The Snake divided in two to go around a couple of islands then came
together wider than before. The next bridge we came to was collapsed
in the center. Cilla gunned the machine and we sailed through the gap.
I could hear cracking noises and turned around to see men standing
on the span. Blooms of light reached out from them as they fired rifles
and shotguns after us.

The sky was lightening all along one bank when Cilla turned the bars and took us up a sloping bank into some stunted pines. She parked the machine in a thick clutch of trees. I started to climb off and she reached back to pat my leg. I sat back down.

She pulled her helmet off and her mask down and sat listening. I listened too. We both sat that way for a long time, the heat of the engine pinging as it cooled under us. The wind moaned soft off the Snake through the pine boughs making the icy ends tinkle against each other. The metal under us popped and hissed as the warmth left it.

Cilla patted my leg again and pulled her rifle from its boot. We climbed off and I followed her with my hand inside the parka holding the butt of the revolver. My yellow parka was now covered over in strips of gray and white duct tape. Cilla said she wouldn't ride with someone who could be seen a mile off and I wasn't giving up the parka. It was waterproof and warm. I also thought it was lucky. That's back when I still believed in luck.

The trees thinned out as we reached the crest of the bank. Past them was a big empty area around a long flat building humped with drifts along its walls. We crouched at the edge of the trees and watched a long time. Nothing moved, nothing changed. Cilla moved out at a dead run and I was behind her the whole way looking back to see if anything stepped out of the tree line. We crossed some animal tracks, caribou or maybe deer, but no boot treads or sled trails.

There was a ghost of a path where Cilla had been here before. It was mostly blown over but I could still see the furrow she made going in and coming out. No other tracks joined or crossed hers. The path led to a space where the drifts were hung up on a section of steel roof leaving a crawlspace underneath. She dropped to hands and knees and bellied into the gap with her rifle cradled in her arms. I went after her and into a dark space. She clutched a handful of my arm and dragged me clear of the hole at the far end.

We were in a dry place where the light from outside came muted through the drifts. I blinked and let my eyes get used to the gloom. Cilla was already moving off deeper into the dark. She lit her oil lamp and I trotted after her shadow to keep up.

The place was big, bigger than Sam's. The lamp's beam never seemed to reach the end of it. The roof was caved in at a lot of places and there were massive pillars of ice grown down to the floor from melting and freezing over all the years. It was old black ice rimed with frost that gleamed like stars when the light of the lamp struck them right. The floor was an uneven landscape of debris covered over with a slick of frost.

It was slow going but Cilla picked the way through for us past the huge pillars and rusting hulks of machinery that towered over us. I tried to make sense of the machines but there was no understanding what they were. They were sheathed in rusted steel and packed with trays of rollers and endless ropes of bundled wire. There were long-dead meters and gauges. I wiped the frost from a few to look through the fogged glass at dials and numbers. None of it meant a damned thing to me. All I had was a sense that these machines made things, big things. Or maybe lots and lots of little things. What any of those things might have been I will never know.

We threaded our way through aisles between the mechanical towers. Cilla stopped at each intersection to shine the light this way or that.

"You're lost," I said.

"I'm not lost. I'm remembering," she said.

After a few bad turns and blind alleys we reached the far wall of the space opposite the way we came in. We stood listening some more. The only sound was the skittering of tiny nails on ice. There were rats here but we never saw any. They must have run ahead of our lamp's beam. And they had tunnels and pathways of their own under the ice-coated junk all over the floor.

"What do they eat," I said in a whisper.

"Us, if we don't keep moving," she said.

She put a hand to the high wall for support and climbed up a jagged slope of tiles and beams where a part of the roof had come down. I picked my way carefully behind her. We came down in a section of the building lined with rows of high shelves like at Sam's but of a heavier construction. There were bins of hardware like washers and bolts and screws. Some had been pulled down and spilled by wasters looking for food or fuel. In the center of the room were stacks of rectangular shapes piled six deep and separated from each other by thick palettes of wood. Some of the taller stacks were collapsed where scavengers shoved them over to get at the palettes for firewood.

The sheets were steel and about the span of one of my arms in width and taller than me in length. I scraped some of the frost away. There was a powdery layer of orange corrosion laying on them but the surface was smooth to the touch beneath that. Even with Cilla's help I couldn't lift a corner of a sheet more than a finger width.

I tapped the top sheet with the butt of my revolver.

"What's that tell you," Cilla said.

"Getting an idea of how hard it is," I said.

"It's fucking hard, that's how hard it is," she said.

"It has to be tool grade or it's no good," I said.

"And this is tool grade."

"I don't know. I don't think so. There's rust on it. I can't be sure."

"We came all this way for nothing," she said.

"I didn't say that. I can tell by how it acts under the torch," I said.

"And you didn't bring the torch along with you, did you, Fingers. Did you."

"Let's look around some more," I said and lifted the lamp high.

There was a set of deep racks against one wall. They held ten-foot lengths of steel bars ranging from the diameter of my finger to the width of my hand. I brushed the frost off the end of one and held the lantern close. There was no sign of corrosion. A fine white powder was there that wiped off on my fingers, leaving a greasy feel.

"This stuff is good," I said.

"You're sure," she said.

"Tool grade. I'm sure of it. No rust. Me and the Boss can lathe these down for the pistons and the rods we need," I said and threw an arm over one to try and haul it off the top of the stack.

"No good," I said.

Cilla threw her arm over the rod and told me to pull. We shifted it maybe an inch clear of the stack.

"There's chains and pulleys and stuff we could use to lift it," I said.

"Then what, Fingers. It's longer than you and me put together. It's not going to fit on the sled even if we could pick it up and carry it," she said.

"All I need is to get it far enough out to cut lengths with the torch. Yay big," I said and held my hands apart maybe four feet.

"And you left the torch in the sled," she said.

"We go out and get it," I shrugged.

"You go out and get it, Fingers. I am staying right here. Tools and all that shit are what you do. You understand that, Fingers," Cilla said.

"Don't call me that. That's not my name."

"Fuck. You. Fingers."

I went outside to get the torch and the tank.

I cursed Cilla the whole way through the woods, dragging that heavy tank behind me up the slope. I had the torch, regulator and hose slung around my shoulders. It was slow going.

I stopped at the edge of the trees to catch my breath.

Ice crackled further down the line of boughs. I crouched, my fist tight on the handle of the revolver tucked against my belly. I lowered my chin to let my breath out down the collar of the parka so it wouldn't show in the air. Along the edge of the broad open space I saw a spray of snow. A deer, a big buck with a velvet thick hide, exploded from the green and made his way bounding over the wide lot to disappear around the far corner of the big building.

I gripped the end of the tank again and started humping it over the crust in the furrow our passage had cut.

That buck. Running on its own. Something made it break from the shelter of the tree line.

I stopped to look back, hood down and breathing slow to hear.

Voices in the trees.

I took the end of the tank and pulled hard for that burrow, taking my time because maybe they didn't know I heard them. Maybe they wanted to see where I was leading them. They knew like I did that no stag ran on its own. There was always a doe somewhere.

I didn't look back. I'd hear the boots on the crusty snow if they moved on me. Just eyes forward for the burrow. Like nothing was wrong and I was alone in the world. Not like there were a hundred hungry eyes watching my back.

My hands were shaking when I shoved the tank ahead of me and crawled in the hole after. Soon as I was out of sight inside the building I stowed the tank and torch to one side. Pistol in my hand I scrambled up and over the ridges of debris on a straight line for the dim glow of the lantern far over the other side of the dark.

When I reached Cilla she had a fire going from some wood she split off a palette and a steel bucket of snow melt bubbling. My lungs burned and I was gasping. She was over to me with a handful of my hair in her fist in seconds. She knew already.

"How many," she said.

"Don't know. Only heard them," I said gasping.

"They see you," she said.

"Couldn't miss me."

She dropped me and took up the steaming pot to drown the fire. There was still a half bucket of melt and she brought that and her rifle along. I snatched up the lamp and followed. She was looking around wildly as we made our way through the tall ranks of shelves for the long back wall. I held the lamp high and saw light bounce off a frame of black metal that climbed the wall.

Steps.

I tapped Cilla's shoulder and pointed the lamp. Steps led up to a boxy kind of room set atop the same kind of steel framework as the shelves. The room was built of sheet steel with grimy black windows all around. She took my arm and pulled me forward up the steps in front of her. My boots rang on the treads as I rushed up. Cilla came behind sloshing water from the bucket as she backed up each step. The melt turned instantly to a rime of ice coating the stairs like paint.

The door to the shack gave under my shoulder and we were both inside. It was a long room with a desk, a table, some chairs and some kind of steel cabinets all down one wall. The floor was a mess of frozen clumps of trash. The musky funk of rat piss cut even through the cold air trapped inside.

Cilla shouldered past me and ran hands over the wall of the shed where it rested against the rear wall of the building. I shone the light and she hissed at me to shut it off. We both ran hands over the bare brick.

"Shit," she said between her teeth.

No door. This was a dead end with no way out. She thought, like I did, that these steps led to another level in another part of the building.

Cilla waved me low and crept back to the door to open it a crack and slip out onto the steel platform. I crouched at the door and we both listened.

There were voices coming out of the dark below. They weren't making any effort to be quiet. They'd followed me in and knew I was still in here somewhere. They knew I was here and I wasn't alone. Cilla came back in on hands and knees and quietly pressed the door closed. There was no latch or lever. Someone popped that out a long time ago. She motioned to me and we went to the big desk. We lifted it from both sides. It was heavy as hell and made of some kind of metal. We placed it tight against the door as quiet as we could.

Next we tried to shift one of the metal cabinets only it was heavier than the desk and the bottom squealed where it ground against the floor. We tried tipping it and a drawer slid out of the face of it to land with a bang on the floor. We crouched in place and listened hard. The voices were still calling to one another but no closer for now. There was no new urgency. They hadn't heard the drawer hitting the floor.

I pulled one of the drawers free. It was filled tight from end to end with stacks of paper. I carried it to the desk against the door and set it down. Cilla pulled another drawer and handed it to me. I stacked it on the other. We went like that, pulling, handing and stacking until we had a pile of the drawers that covered the door and weighed down the desk. We slid more underneath to create a complete wall to block the door.

Some rats boiled out of one of the drawers where they'd made a cozy nest of chewed papers. Cilla dropped the drawer to the floor. The greasy bastards spilled to the floor and vanished into the shadows.

Locked in tight, we moved low to peep from the bottom of the windows. The glare of flames sputtered out there on the other side of one of the huge ice columns. They were hunting for us using torches of some kind.

"We shouldn't have holed up here. We should have run. Found another way out," Cilla said hushed.

"Might not be another way out. They might know this place better than us. Be waiting for us outside," I said.

"I don't think so. I've been away three days. No sign on the snow. No sign anyone's been in here in a long time. They heard the machine and followed the sound," she said.

"Then followed me," I said.

"You are a fuck up, Fingers," she said and I was hurt and angry at that. I looked her in the eye to tell her to go to hell. She was smiling.

"Yeah. That's me," I said shrugging.

She clapped a hand on her mouth and then my own to keep us from laughing out loud.

T hat's how it is sometimes. Someone's out there in the dark sharpening their knives for your ass and none of it seems real. It strikes you as funny. You have to laugh because you can only be tired and hungry and scared so long.

Cilla was never anything but a pure bitch to me. Always treating me like a dumb kid she was stuck with. That moment was the first time I saw her drop the mask and act like a person. Course, it was over me admitting I was a fuck up. I guess it was something we could both agree on.

And like it or not, we were likely to die together in that little room at the top of those steps.

The voices came closer with the light of the torches. We could hear them shoving aside junk looking for me, looking for anyone.

Quiet as rats, quieter, Cilla and me lifted the ends of the long table and carried it to the wall of windows. She found some folded tarps. We covered ourselves with a tarp to hide our shape so we could lean on the table and see out over the bottom frame of the windows.

Men came into view. I counted eight by the time they'd all stepped clear of the surrounding black. They ranged over the dark floor of the factory in pools of light from torches held high. The lights guttered and threw crazy shadows all over, making it look like there were hundreds of them out there. One of them sniffed out the still steaming fire. We watched him stick his hand in the embers and yank it back quick. He whistled for the others and they ran to join him.

We couldn't catch a lot of what they said. We didn't need to.

They wore layers of animal skins rough-sewn together. I saw buckskin and dog. They all carried weapons but only two had rifles or shotguns covered in hide sleeves. The rest had knives, axes and one carried a long handled mallet. They were all grown men. No kids. No women. Either that was their make-up or they were scouts. If that was so they'd have the rest of their band travelling behind.

The bunch broke up and hunted around, leaving one man behind. The torches separated to spread out into the gloom. The guy left back was using an ax to break up and split strips of wood off a palette. He built a fire on the floor, lighting it with a striking stick on some paper he tore out of a book that was hidden somewhere on him. He got it going hot and bright and stripped off his outer layer of skins. Underneath he wore ragged cloth clothes and leggings of patched-together skins. They were of some kind of hairless brown leather. I wasn't sure what it was until I saw dark markings on the skins.

Tattoos.

They were man-hunters.

In the shimmer of the fire I could see the guy's face. His skin was waxy and his eyes set way back in his head like they'd retreated into his skull. His teeth were black with rot. His hair hung in greasy patches from his skull. Around his neck were bones strung on a thong. Finger bones ranging in size from long adult fingers to tiny baby ones.

It wasn't funny anymore. I could feel Cilla close by me under the tarp. She was shivering. It wasn't the cold.

We watched the guy pull a flank of meat out of a pack and put it on the floor. It was wrapped in filthy paper. He took a thin-bladed knife from a sheath on his belt and cut strips from it. He searched around the floor and found a battered sheet of metal that he placed by the fire. He let it rest there a while before hawking a gobbet of spit to watch it sizzle away. Then he set the strips side by side until they bled some fat. He poked and turned them with a knife to keep them from sticking.

Dinner cooking, he looked around him to see what else he could find. That's when he spied the stairs leading up to our hide. He licked his fingers, stood up, and made his way through the mess for the bottom of the stairs.

I heard the muted click of Cilla drawing back the hammer on her Winchester she held close. I pulled my revolver clear, slow and quiet. We couldn't see the guy anymore but we could hear his boots on the steps as he moved closer to us.

A high cry was followed by a series of impacts we could feel vibrating through the walls of the shack. Then a voice called out all trembling and pained.

The son of a bitch slipped on the ice and fell backward down the stairs. The water Cilla poured there as we climbed to the hide.

The voice rose higher. Calling out a name.

"Sy! Sy! I'm hurt, Sy!"

Torches bobbed in the dark, coming closer. Four of the men returned from their hunt back to the fire. We could hear the fallen man crying out for them. The men moved out of sight to where the man lay at the bottom of the stairs. He was begging and pleading with them in a wheedling voice.

They laughed at him.

He screamed. We could see them haul the guy closer to the fire. They dumped him on the floor where he rolled on his side clutching at his leg. One leg below the knee was turned at angle that hurt to look at. He held one of his arms bent close to his chest. The biggest of the men, one of the guys who had a rifle, gave orders to the others.

I watched as long as I could. The fallen guy was screaming and crying as they whipped a line tight around his ankles. He was calling to Sy, reaching out his fingers to the biggest man who stood by watching. They hooked the line through a brace of the frame that supported our hide. The fallen man shrieked as they hauled him from the floor. We could feel the vibration of his struggling weight being drawn up under us. The big man and two of the others stepped back while the fourth stepped out of sight below where we could see.

The shriek turned to a stuttering gurgle. A fine spray of blood showered the floor and steamed there until it froze black. The four men walked back to the fire to share the strips of meat scorching there on the steel plate. We could hear the squeak squeak squeak of the rope as the dead man swung below us bleeding out.

The three other men came back from their search to join the rest at the fire. Pretty soon five more came in through the dark. They'd been waiting outside, I guess. Watching for whoever might run out. They gave up on the hunt. They had their meat.

They didn't know it but they had us too.

T he men were noisy and night-blind from being close to the fire they kept burning with fresh wood spilt off the palettes.

That freed Cilla and me to move around a little. We ate some caribou jerky and shared the little bit of melt water that was left in the pot. We searched around the hide in the flicker of the light from below, opening drawers and poking under debris. Cilla made a kind of bed of layered papers under the table. I found a half-empty glass bottle in the back of a drawer. It had a spread-wing bird with two heads on the faded paper label. It looked like water and tasted like gasoline. I choked and slapped a hand over my mouth. Cilla took the bottle from me and had a short swallow then whispered to me to lay off it. She didn't give the bottle back to me.

I lay up on the table to hide under the tarp and keep watch. Cilla lay on the bed of papers under the table and was soon asleep. We were going to have to wait them out, hope they'd fill their bellies with their late friend and move on.

They showed no signs of doing that. They made themselves comfortable around the fire, taking turns sleeping and scavenging. They quartered their former friend and wrapped the parts in sheets of paper they found somewhere.

The liver and heart they roasted on spits. The scent of them cooking rose through the seams of the metal walls of our hide. The smell made my mouth water. I couldn't help it. Meat is meat. Food is food. No matter what we tell ourselves differently.

Their diet took its toll on them though. Too much of any one thing is bad. I met a man once who ate nothing but rabbits. Raised them from birth in litters just for himself. He wasted away even though his belly was always full. He went blind before he died, looking like an old man even though he had only a few years on me. Could have been something other than having rabbit for every meal. But that was the only constant in his life.

The man-eaters all seemed sick. They coughed and hacked and spat. I could hear them complaining of having watery guts. Their skin leggings were all shit-stained from having the runs. I watched a guy pull a tooth from his own mouth easy as plucking a hair. He flicked it into the fire.

I must have dozed and woke up to men laughing and not knowing where I was. Had to remind myself to stay still. Even fire-blind, these bastards might spot a quick movement above them. Cilla and me had to be careful not to cast shadows.

From under the tarp I watched the men gather around the fire. I squinted to see what they were so damned pleased about. The big man reached into the fire with a long bladed knife and pulled back a human skull scorched black. He set it by the fire and tapped the bone hard with the butt of the knife then used the point to jab and pry the crown open. A cloud of vapor rose from the widening crack. The big man dug the point inside and came up with a steaming glob of pink meat. It was broiled brain.

The others took a share of the slimy meat making happy sounds like kids. I tasted the jerky and vodka in my mouth again.

WINTERWORLD ❋ CHUCK DIXON

T here was no light from outside we could see to tell us if it were
day or night.

We took turns sleeping and watching and lost all sense of how many
hours passed. Time went along at its own pace.

I have no idea if we were sleeping too much or too little. I felt drowsy
and never fully awake all the time. Maybe it was the closed space. Or
the smoky heat rising up to us from the big fire. The only way I knew
a lot of time had passed, more than a day anyway, was my hunger.

We had some jerky and hard candy and parceled it out as best we
could. But it wasn't enough and it wasn't going to last. The water was
gone so we shared the vodka in tiny sips. It only made us more thirsty.

And we waited.

It seemed to me that these guys weren't going to move out until they'd
finished every scrap of their friend. I was glad he was the smallest of them.
Twelve guys, by my count, couldn't take too long to choke him down.

I was hard asleep under the table, head buzzing from an empty stomach and a head full of vodka, when I felt a something close by me.

I went to sit up and, forgetting where I was, hit my head on the bottom of the table. A hand pressed me back down on the bed of papers.
It was Cilla. She'd crawled under the table with me. Her hand stayed
where it was. Her face close to mine.

"Scully," she said.

I was asking what was going on when she pressed her mouth on
mine and kept it there.

I don't want Wynn to know this part so I'm writing it in my own hand.

If you're reading this I've been dead a long time.

It won't read like Flowbear that's for damn sure.

She talked me into telling my story and I'm not sure why I'm going along with it. Most of this shit I don't want to remember. Most of it I thought I forgot until she started pestering me and I started talking.

But since I started I want to tell the whole thing. Even the parts I'd rather not say out loud to Wynn.

That night under that table with a pack of cannibals eating one of their own just a few feet below us is one night I think about a lot. I wonder what I should of done. I wonder if I ever had a choice. Like your stomach clenching when you smell meat you know you shouldn't want but you want it anyway. The body betrays the mind. Whatever you thought you knew about yourself turns out to be lies.

Cilla lay on top of me and kissed me. We were close in size only she was a grown woman. Grown in years maybe only a few years older than me but I still felt like a kid. I guess she didn't feel that way. Or maybe it was the vodka. I never did see the bottle again.

I say I felt like a kid but there's where the body turns the mind into a liar again. I was sprouting hair in places where there'd been none and had been doing so for awhile. And I'd been looking at Cilla a lot more than before especially when she didnt think I could see her. And I woke up a few times in the night dreaming about her but she was a different Cilla and looked at me in a way she never looked at me when I was awake.

Like she was looking at me now where we lay close together under that table.

She kept kissing me, moving her mouth from my mouth to my neck and her hands working to loosen my clothes. Before I knew what I was doing I was kissing her back and my hands were reaching under her clothes and feeling her warm skin on my fingers.

Well you either got to be one dumb or one sick son of a bitch to need me to tell you what happened next.

I will only say that it was damned hard to keep quiet up in that hide but we managed.

And one last thing, it's one thing to know you want something. It's a whole nother thing to find out how much you need it.

Cilla talked to me, kept talking to me, lying close in the smoky dark.

"We're going to get out of here," she said.

"I know," I said. I said it but I wasn't sure I believed it.

Then what. "We go back to the Garage, to the Boss," she said.

"The Boss and me make the parts. Take the Leviathan to Mechanicsburg. Like we planned all this time," I said.

"That's bullshit. You know that, right. That's a crazy old man talking," she said.

"It's his machine, Cilla. We go where he wants even if it is bullshit."

"His machine. What did he do. You did the work. You and Fingers before you. Without you and me he'd never be able to feed himself."

"His machine, Cilla. His fuel. We go where he says. What else we going to do. Where else we going to go."

"There's a place past the end of the Snake way the other side of the Big Ice. It's warm there. Open water like back in the days. Ground that's not covered by ice. The people barely wear any clothes at all," she said with a heat in her eyes I never saw there before.

"You've seen this place," I said.

"I know it's there. I seen pictures. Even a map."

"The Boss won't go there," Cilla.

"We go without him," she said.

I started to answer. She covered my mouth with hers. She ground her body against me.

I pushed her away. She grabbed my head in her hands and forced her face back close to mine.

"He's old, Scully. How much longer can he live. He's not strong enough to make it out here. That's why he has me. And you. We're young. We're strong. We need to take the chances we get."

"How far can we get on the ski machine," I said.

"We take the Leviathan when you finish it," she said.

"We just take his machine and leave him to die," I said.

"No. We'd make sure he was dead before we left," she said.

I pushed her away and got out from under the table. She tried to talk more and I covered my ears with my hands. She couldn't raise her voice. I didn't want her words in my head. I didn't want her hands on me anymore. Only it's not like I had anywhere to go.

That bitch worked on me. She kept talking to me, daring me and baiting me.

She had no heart. I could see that but I couldn't keep away. No heart but all heat. I don't know how many times we laid down together under that table.

I'd wake up with her lying on me, skin to skin, and be too weak to push her away. She disgusted me almost as much as I disgusted myself.

When she wasn't touching and kissing and pressing herself to me she'd talk.

What she said scared me more than what was waiting outside that door and down those steps.

It scared me because I was starting to listen. I was starting to think of the days ahead with me and her together in the Leviathan rolling out onto the Big Ice looking for this place she swore she could find.

The Boss might even be dead by the time we got out of this shithole back to the Garage.

I started thinking that would make it easier. If we found him dead just like the old man and mother and the two little kids back in the warm hole. It would be easy.

Then I started hoping he'd be dead.

That scared me most of all.

S he told me I didn't know the Boss. She told me he wasn't what he acted like he was, all kind and giving. She told me she'd been with him since she was younger, just a kid he found cold and starving on the banks of the Snake.

Sure, he took her in and fed her. But he did more than that. He used her like he owned her. Used her like a woman though she was only a girl. Did it for years until he got too old and crippled in the hands and body. She got old enough to say no and back it up. That's why she spent so much time away from the Garage. That's why she had her own place she could lock behind her.

"He'd still be doing me if he didn't get all shriveled up. Shriveled up everywhere," she said with a bitter smile.

"I don't believe that," I said. I didn't want to believe it was the truth.

"Think I'd lie," Cilla said.

"You said there were other people. They touch you too, make you do things," I said.

Her eyes flashed and she got up to pull her clothes back on.

I knew then it wasn't true. I knew not to believe anything she said.

I reached a hand out to brush my fingers down the bare skin of her leg, to touch the warmth there. She knocked my hand away and stepped out of reach.

I was dead in her eyes. As dead as the Boss.

The man-eaters pissed on the fire and walked away into the dark. We watched the jogging light of their torches for a long time. They climbed over and around the heaps of debris and around the shining pillars of ice. I pressed my ear to the dirty glass and listened. The quiet closed in as dense as the dark.

We waited more, staring through the glass into the blackness outside. Looking for any glimmer or movement that would mean they only meant to trick us into exposing ourselves. Cilla was the first to lose patience with it and pulled down the barricade of drawers. I helped and we pitched them to the floor as fast as we could. To hell with the noise. If they heard it they'd come running and we needed to get out of there anyway.

Together we dragged the big desk aside. The sudden effort made me dizzy. I was dehydrated and my stomach was empty. I focused on following Cilla out of there. She held the lamp up in one hand and the rifle in the other. She was surrounded by a swirling tunnel of darkness. I reached out to steady myself with a hand on her shoulder. She shrugged it off.

I tested the steps with my boot. They were dry. The ice that rimed them before melted in the heat of the man-eaters' cook fire. We made it off the steps. Cilla went to the cold cook fire. I followed, stepping over bones scattered all around. I looked back. A pair of feet and the broken end of a leg bone still dangled there from the steel frame under our hide. Cilla reached into a place under one of the big steel racks and came back with her leather pack still buckled closed.

"Those fuckers didn't find it," she said.

She dug in it handing me a candy bar while she cut open a can of beans with her clasp knife. Cilla snuffed the flame in the lamp. We moved into the deeper shadows between two standing racks. We crouched there listening and eating. I split the candy bar with her. It melted in my mouth enough to chew. When that was done we took turns scooping cold beans from the can with our fingers.

There were no sounds or lights anywhere.

Cilla got up to leave and I grabbed her arm. She pulled it away but I grabbed it again and yanked her to a stop.

"Where are you going," I said.

"I'm getting out of here," she said.

"We still need to get what we came for, Cilla."

"Hell with it. They might come back."

"More likely they're waiting outside. They know someone was in here. They know there's only one way out."

She thought on that and nodded.

We moved together through the dark. She took two strips of tape off my parka and covered the lens of the lamp until only a slit of light shone through. It was enough to help us see our way without throwing off a glare.

The tank, hoses and cutting torch were still where I left them just inside the doorway. The gang of wasters thought they were just more junk if they noticed them at all. We hefted both ends of the tank and carried it back to the racks. I had the hose and the torch looped over my shoulder. The regulator was in Cilla's pack.

There was still no shifting those heavy tool steel rods. Especially not with both of us as weak as we were from being hungry. I climbed up into the rack atop the pile of rods. It was tight and I had to bend double but there was enough room to cut off a section of rod at a time. I fired up the torch and dialed the gas mix to make a fine cutting flame.

Cilla moved away from the glaring light and into the surrounding darkness to keep watch. I pulled on my thick welding goggles and followed a line I'd eyeballed and set the point of the flame to the steel. It took a while but the heat trapped under the rack was a bonus. It got hot enough in there I had to take the parka off. I was starting to sweat heavy under my coverall. That sweat would leech heat from my skin when I went back out to the cold.

I had a two-foot length cut off and kicked it clear of the stack to fall to the floor. By the time I cut five more the same length I was down to my USA t-shirt and it was sopping. I cut the gas and the torch went out to let the dark flood in around me again. A whistle brought a returning pair of whistles from out in the gloom. Cilla was there with the lamp as I was stripping off the t-shirt. I tried to use it to towel off the rest of the sweat turning to frost on my skin. I pulled the coverall back up and zipped it closed, then the parka. The chills set in and I banged my hands on my arms to bring the circulation on.

We shared another candy bar. We sipped water from a steel jug that I'd set close to me on the rack to let the heat from the cutting torch thaw it. Cilla opened a can of some kind of fish and we forked pieces out with our knives.

"You know what I was saying before," she said.

"I don't want to talk," I said.

"I was scared, crazy with fear. You know. I didn't mean any of that. I didn't mean what I said."

I didn't answer. Just speared another flake of fish out of the can.

"It was talk, Scully. Just talk. To make the time go."

"Was it all to make the time go by," I said.

She looked at me, lips parted. Then she smiled and lowered her head, her eyes hooded.

"Not all of it, Scully. I mean, we can keep on like that, anytime you want."

"You and me," I said.

"Who else," she said, dropping her face into shadow to pluck a bit of meat off the tip of her knife with her lips.

"Yeah, who else," I shrugged like it was a silly question.

E ven cut to shorter lengths like they were the steel rods were
heavy. It took both of us to move them. It was hard work over
the rough ground of the factory floor. We picked out the easiest
route and made six trips out to the doorway that we entered from
and five back to the racks. We took a rest between trips three and
four. The water was still liquid. We shared the jug until it was dry
then made the trips with the last of the rods.

The revolver in my hand, I went out the doors to the tunnel. There
was no light coming through the drifts. I crawled to the end, to just a
few feet shy of the outside. It was dead-of-night dark outside with a
thick, swirling snow falling. Big fat flakes building on the crust.

"Perfect," Cilla said when I told her.

"No light and the snow to cover any noise," I said.

We hurried to take the six rod sections and slide them across the icy
floor of the tunnel and out into the night. It was hard work but easier
than carrying them. We took turns shoving them up the slick floor of
the tunnel ahead of us.

"You wait here, Scully. I go for the machine and we load the sled,"
she said.

I nodded. Cilla went to leave then turned back to touch my face and
kiss me hard. She dropped her face mask down and ran into the churn-
ing white with the rifle in her fists.

It wasn't long before I heard the whine of the ski machine growing
closer. In the thick snowfall it was hard to tell what direction it was
coming from. It sounded like it was moving away then the grind of it

got louder and harsher. Cilla came out of the waves of falling white, the light of the headlamp slicing a path in the night. She slid to a halt and dismounted.

"They didn't leave. The wasters," she said.

I strained to look for the tree line invisible through the whiteout.

"I led them away but they'll find us again," she said.

I kept watching the trees, thinking this might be a story she was telling me.

No time for that, she said and set the rifle down to help me load sections of rod into the bed of the sled.

We got them on board and climbed onto the ski machine. We heard a muffled thump from somewhere in the dark. A spray of snow kicked up in front of us. The man-eaters were here. She told me the truth. They were close enough to see us now.

Cilla turned the controls on the handle bars and the machine leapt forward only to jerk to a stop that threw us both forward.

"The sled," I said.

"It's too damn heavy," she said and swung a leg to climb off the bench.

"You keep the engine revving. We need to break out the sled," she called and put her hands to the sled to push.

I slid forward and turned the handlebar controls forward like I'd seen her do a hundred times. The engine throbbed under me. The machine moved this way and that like an animal fighting against a harness. I looked back to see her pushing, her eyes wide and staring past me through the holes in her mask. She was shouting but I couldn't hear words over the howling machine.

I turned to see black shapes humping out of the gloom at the end of the headlamp beam. One of them was Sy, waving an ax over his head as he jogged for us.

The machine jumped under me and slewed through the fresh powder at a severe angle. With a tug I righted the handlebars and set it on a straight course, the sled hissing over the white surface behind me. I looked back to see Cilla trotting after me, calling out with the rifle over her head. I turned the machine then to run parallel to the ragged rank of wasters rushing for us. Cilla changed course to follow me, lifting her feet to clear the snow. I gunned the engine and powered away without looking back.

I remember her calling my name over and over. That's impossible because I couldn't have heard anything over the roar of the big six-stroke under me.

Skis up, I crashed into the trees with the sled banging brush behind me. Snow and ice dropped on me from branches above, blinding me as I looked for the slope down to the Snake. I was away from the reach of the man-eaters so I eased off the throttle a bit. This was my first time actually driving the machine. All I knew about its operation was from watching Cilla. The hand and foot controls either revved too hard or brought me down to a rattling idle. I had no time to learn the finer points. I had to get out on flat ice without tipping the sled and make some distance. Slowing to pick a path through the trees dropped the noise of the engine to a dull thrum.

The boom of gunfire reached me through the trees behind me. Booms followed by a rapid stream of flat cracks. Cilla was back there working that rifle. There was another boom. I didn't hear the Winchester again.

I powered the machine through the last of the trees and broke out onto the Snake to turn the bars to the right for home.

It was hard. I worked it out in my head. I traded one life for two. Cilla for me and the Boss.

Cilla was never going to let me live to see the Garage again after she said what she said to me. I saw the fire in her eyes. That fire doesn't lie. It comes from somewhere deep inside. It had been building in Cilla a long time.

That didn't make it any easier to do what I did. Doesn't make it any easier to talk about it either.

And then, who's sitting here telling you this story.

G etting back to the Garage took a while longer than the trip out. Dragging the heavy sled behind me the whole way cut my speed. And I had to stay on the ice pack. No side trips up the banks to avoid the bridges. Too much danger of the sled tipping on rough ground. I'd never be able to right it on my own.

I made a dead run of it with no stops. The last part of it I don't remember at all.

I reached the tunnel gate and the chains were in place with the big lock closed. I forgot all about the key. Cilla kept it on her. All I could do was bang on the bars and holler. The Boss came out of the dark after a long time with bolt cutters under his arm. He handed the cutters through to me and I snipped the hasp of the lock off. I was wasted. It took my full weight pressed on the handle to make the cut.

The Boss replaced the chains and I snapped on a fresh lock after I motored the ski machine into the tunnel.

"Cilla," he said.

All I could do was shake my head. I couldn't look into his eyes. I couldn't trust what I might say. He threw his arms around me, patted my head.

"Get inside and warm up. Get some sleep," he said.

I guess I made it to my bunk because that's where I woke up later still in all my clothes.

The Boss had some kind of soup waiting for me. I drained four bowls. Then I went down to the still where it was warmer and stripped off my clothes. I dumped two buckets of hot water over me and scrubbed my skin red with rags I found in a barrel by the still fire.

I dressed and used a cart to haul the steel rods into the work area. The Boss looked at the rods, running the backs of his fingers over them. He looked at the cuts I burned in them with a jeweler's glass.

"They'll do. There's more than enough to make the parts we need," he said.

I tried to smile. I didn't make it.

"Tell me, son," he said.

"It was wasters, Boss. They caught us coming out of where we found the steel. Too many of them," I said. It was all true for what it was.

He put a hand to my shoulder before turning away.

There was no way I was telling him everything. Let him pine for Cilla all he wanted. Where was the benefit in telling him what a scheming bitch she was. Let him believe the lie that she gave a shit about him. And I'd believe the lie that I felt right about leaving her behind.

The Boss got drunk and stayed that way for the next two days. He was mostly in his bunk passed out or close to it. I needed his help machining the new parts. Or maybe I didn't. Maybe I just didn't feel like doing anything either.

After a day of tending the still I got restless. I took the bolt cutters and snipped the lock off of the door to Cilla's container. I'd never been in there. No one had but her. Now it was the only thing left of her and I wanted to see it.

There was an oil lamp by the door. I lit and scanned the interior. There were more lamps bolted up on the walls. I lit them too. It wasn't much inside. She'd insulated the walls and floor with layer after layer of blankets, quilts, carpet and whatever else she could find on her trips out. There were clothes and empty bottles scattered on the floor. Piles of magazines were stacked against a wall. There were fancy boxes stuffed with jewelry on top of a cabinet. I pulled open the drawers but there was nothing inside but a mess of socks, ammo for her rifle and tiny bottles full of stuff that smelled sharply sweet. At the rear end of the container was a bunk overhung with thick curtains strung up there to hold in her heat while she slept.

I parted the curtains and climbed into her bunk and lay there smelling her scent. I held the pillow to my nose and breathed in the dried sweat infused in the cloth. It brought her back to me. I could almost feel her lying close and warm next to me. Hear her sweet words of murder and promises of love.

Laying back all stretched out I could see something shimmering above me in the light. I reached for my lamp on me and held it above me.

Pasted on the ceiling of the bunk were hundreds of pictures cut or torn from magazines. They all shared a theme. They all had happy people in them standing by open water or in the water swimming or riding on boats. They stood and sat on something that looked like snow but couldn't be since none of them were wearing boots. None of them were wearing much at all. Women waved their hands with just enough on to cover their asses and breasts. Guys were holding up drinks in tall glasses. Kids ran through the waves. Everywhere were these tall trees with leaves only at the top and colorful birds flew between them. Tall white buildings lined the shore under clear skies and bright sun. Even in the pictures taken at night it looked warm with people in shirts with sleeves that didn't cover their arms and pants that didn't reach their knees. No one wore gloves or boots. They danced and laughed and kissed and looked like they never went hungry or thirsty or knew what it was to be bone cold and afraid.

Cilla would lay here just like I was. She'd look up at these pictures and imagine herself there with all those cheerful assholes. She'd think about her toes in the warm water or holding hands with some guy in the shade of the trees. Cilla would fall asleep every night looking up at a world she wanted to be a part of no matter what it took to get her there. She probably dreamed about it every night and woke up in her shitty steel box with nothing to look forward to except rooting around in whatever the dead left behind years and years ago.

My throat felt like something was pinching it closed. My eyes burned. I got out of there and just ran. I ran down the tunnels into the dark. I ran until my sides hurt and my mouth was numb from sucking cold air. When I couldn't run any more I fell on my knees and wept into my fists until I was dry.

The Boss sobered up, mostly, and we got to work.

I threw myself into it. I needed something else to think about. Machining the new rods and pistons would take up all the space in my head. The work left me too tired to think about anything else when I lay down to sleep.

It was frustrating and tedious. The tolerances were unforgiving. There was one join I drilled out three times, wasting a lot of the tool steel before getting it right. If I kept up like this I'd have to go back for more tool stock. That was the last place I'd ever want to return to. And I've left some real bad places behind me in my roaming.

The Boss showed me the finer points of using a micrometer. Making those pistons fit the cylinders used almost invisible variances. It was slow work, nervous work. I never thought we'd get Leviathan moving. There was no room in my imagination for the idea that something that big would ever function. Not if it relied on my efforts.

The old man told me to keep faith in my own abilities. A good mechanic had to believe in his work and his solutions. My confidence was like a weak flame inside me. I only looked at the work in front of me. I couldn't maintain the idea that every little laborious task would lead to that monster machine coming to life.

I only stopped working the lathes to go to Sam's. We needed to stock up on goods for our eventual departure for Mechanicsburg. That's the excuse I used anyway. I needed time away from the workshop. And I really needed time away from the old man. The truth was burning a hole in me and I was afraid I'd tell him everything about Cilla. I had no idea how he'd feel about what I'd done. I didn't want to find out.

Without anyone there to rush me I spent whole days at Sam's. I explored every corner of the place. I took a half dozen lamps with me and left them spotted around to mark my path in and out. I turned them on as I entered and off as I left. It made the place a little less scary. The lamps threw the shadows of rats high up on the walls whenever they crossed the beam. In addition to rats I found raccoons living in a tribe inside what was once a walk-in freezer. Now the insulated walls kept out the cold. There must have been fifty or more of them in there. My lamp beam picked out their eyes, glowing red, from the dark in shimmering constellations.

I stayed away from that section. Raccoons can get big and they're always nasty if you get close to their young. I guess that goes for all animals except man. As long as I kept to my side of Sam's they kept to theirs.

As much time as Sam's had been here empty there was still a lot to pick from. No one else had found it lying here under a shelf of snow and ice. Except the animals, of course. It was a race against rot and rust for the goodies, though. I mostly gathered up canned goods that looked okay and took along the last sacks of rice that hadn't been clawed open. That meant unloading the palettes to reach the sacks at the center of the pile. I took along palettes too to use for the still fire.

The work was hard and I'd take time away to wander the big empty cave of a place. I found the USA shirts again and took the five that fit me along with a few more bags of socks. The rest of the clothes were useless. Shirts with flowers printed on them and short pants with lots of pockets and small pants in all kinds of crazy colors that cinched at the belly with a string. I saw those pants on some of the men in the pictures Cilla had in her bunk. There were bathing suits for women on plastic hangers and hats made of straw with paper flowers on them all covered over with a dusting of frost. If Cilla were here she'd be grabbing some of that stuff up to wear when we got to that paradise she was looking for. I thought of how she might look in one of those skimpy swimming suits. First I pictured her still in her boots and that made me smile, sat there giggling like an idiot. I closed my eyes and breathed easy and I could see her there with those happy people in the pictures wearing just enough to cover her ass; feet bare in the toasty warm sand. She was smiling, a drink in her hand, at something one of the men said. She had a hand up to shade her eyes from the sun. I could hear her chuckling in her throat over the sound of the ice tinkling in the glass and the surf rumbling in behind her.

A real rumble reached me. My eyes shot open. Somewhere past the reach of the lamps something fell from one of the high shelves. It hit every surface coming down. The sound of it echoed and re-echoed through the place. I pulled the revolver and ducked down to hide in the rack of hanging clothes. I crouched there a long time with ears straining and listening for more noises. Or voices.

The last of the sounds died with a crunching noise. Whatever fell off that high place crushed something under it when it finally came to rest. The silence fell over the place again. Could have been a carton shoved off a ledge by a raccoon. Could just have been a shelf giving way to time and decay.

I crouched and listened for more sounds to follow. There was always the chance someone would find this place. We were ten miles from the closest collection of people in either direction along the Snake. They could be scrounging this far out. Or a nomad band might come across Sam's. I stared into the black and imagined I saw movement there. A gang of man-eaters like back at the factory. Or ragmen up from that bridge. Or the one person who knew about this place all along.

Cilla.

I didn't see her die. I couldn't be sure. She could have retreated back into that factory and hid out from those cannibals until they got tired of looking. Maybe they took her alive and she escaped. If she walked back here it would take days and days to reach the Garage. I was figuring the numbers in my head. Had enough time passed. I couldn't recall how long I'd been back. It seemed to me plenty of time for someone on foot to reach Sam's from the factory. And this is where she'd come first. This is where she could wait for me, knowing I'd come.

Hidden down among the colorful summer clothes, I could feel her eyes searching the dim light for my shadow. I held a hand over my mouth to stop my breath being seen. I could imagine her up on one of the high shelves training the front tang of the Winchester's sights down on me. That's what I convinced myself of, she knocked something loose climbing to a sniper's roost. That's what I heard falling. Cilla was perched up over me waiting for me to move so she could put a bullet in me.

"Cilla," I called out.

"I'm sorry. I'm so sorry," I called.

The silence was like a weight pressing me down.

"I couldn't let you kill the old man."

No sound anywhere. Just me breathing.

I rose to my feet, showing myself to anyone out there in the dark watching.

Dead silence.

There was no one there. I was alone.

"Asshole," I said to myself.

I gathered my loot in sacks and carried them away, killing the flame in the lamps as I retraced my path back to the hole in the wall and out. All the way out of Sam's and through the scrub pines in the gully I could feel eyes on me. When I finally got back to the Garage my shoulders burned with pain. Not from carrying the sacks of loot, from tensing in expectation of a bullet in the back.

T he big sixteen roared to life then died with a coughing sound. I
sat up in the control cabin, my hand on the gearshift. The Boss
whooped.

"Give her another crank," he was shouting, grinning so big I could
see it even through that beard of his.

I worked the hand crank bolted on the central console. The machine
was built back when they used batteries to power the starter. There
hadn't been a reliable working battery since before the Boss was born.
We used the crank for ignition. It was the best way to feed juice to an
engine the size of the Leviathan.

I cranked and fed her diesel.

"Slow, slow," the Boss said.

The engine clunked and stuttered and I eased my foot off the pedal.
The idle steadied and became regular and strong. The cabin rocked
with the vibration.

"Holy shit," I said.

"What's that," the Boss said, calling over the rumble.

"HOLY SHIT," I shouted.

He grinned and made motion to shoo me over. I clambered over the
center console into the passenger seat and the Boss took my place at
the wheel. He rested those misshapen old hands on the steering wheel
and felt the pulse of the Leviathan's heart rise up his arms. There were
tears in his eyes when he turned to me.

"All these years. All these years. I never thought I'd see this day. I
never thought the goddamned thing would actually work," he said.

"I thought you had faith," I said.

"I had bullshit, son. That's what I had," he said.

He laid his forehead on the throbbing wheel and his body shook with laughter. I laughed even though my eyes were wet with tears too. I don't know what I was feeling. Maybe it was all the hard work paying off, seeing those days and days of labor and risk come to something as the big monster of a truck purred pure power from its engine compartment. That was part of it, I guess. Looking back, thinking on it now, I understand that I was happy, actually happy. Not so much for myself as I was for the old man. He was the closest thing I had in the world to someone I could trust. And he trusted me and that meant even more.

You can go this whole world over from end to end, searching and scrounging and picking over the little that's left for us. You know the rarest thing you can find, if you can ever find it. That's someone you can turn your back on, someone you can shut your eyes to. That trusting, that knowing, is the hardest thing to come by because that's what man has been brought down to. He's a grasping, hungry animal when the cold and the want comes for him. The rats, those raccoons nested in that deep freezer, have more of a sense of reliance than most men or women I've run into. They'll die to protect their own. All we do is kill to have enough warmth to make it through the night or enough food to make it through another day.

Right at that moment, I loved that old man. I know now that's what it was. I'd do anything for him and never look back.

But I'd never tell him about Cilla.

And that hurt me because I knew I could trust the Boss only he didn't know he'd never be able to trust me because I could never share the truth with him. That truth, that I left Cilla to die, would cause him to look at me differently. He might even agree with what I'd done but that wouldn't stop him wondering and worrying over it. I'd lose some of that bond between us.

That was the one line I could not cross.

We winched the Leviathan up and I used the ski-machine to haul the tread wheels into place. I had them mounted back in place in two long days of work. It was tough doing it by myself, working the winch then checking the position of the frame and having to work the winch some more and back and forth until each tread wheel was in position to be bolted back on.

The Boss joined me up in the cabin as I cranked her to start. He instructed me on how to use the clutch and shifters. It took a few tries, a few stalls and more cranking but I got that monster moving in gear. We trundled up the wide tunnel in low, the big treads biting into the concrete floor. We were both screaming like crazy men fit to burst with pride.

I backed her up and turned into the tunnel where the still sat. I left the Boss in the cabin while I climbed down the ladder for the hose. I secured it in place in the opening of the two-thousand-liter tank. I'd mounted in it a metal cage I welded together to hold it. It rested slung behind the engine housing. Working the hand pump, I got a flow going and loaded the tank to the brim with alcohol.

We pulled the big machine back into the work area where the old man could climb out onto the scaffold and down.

The next couple of days we spent loading goods into the insulated compartments. We stuffed every inch with cans of food and plastic buckets of noodles and rice. I filled the fifty-gallon tank with purified water. It would rest inside the engine housing where it would stay thawed. We crammed the small sleeping compartment at the back of the driver's cabin with spare clothes, boots, medicines, a case of Jack, tools, and the manuals for the sixteen-cylinder for when we'd need to work on it. There was barely room for one of us to sleep at a time in there. But there'd be more room as we used up some of the supplies.

The Boss did the numbers and figured we had a range of almost a thousand miles with the fuel we had. He was sure we'd find more as we rode even if we didn't find Mechanicsburg on the first tank. I wasn't comfortable with that estimate so I filled thirty cans with the diesel we had. I strapped them down wherever I could find room on the Leviathan's shell.

We had no idea how far this place was. I still wasn't convinced it was any more real than Cilla's dreams of a place where you didn't need a fire to stay warm. I wasn't sure what it was I was looking for. I was only excited about getting this monster of ours out on the ice and going anywhere we wanted to take it. If we never found Mechanicsburg I'd be fine with that, so long as we could find or make enough fuel to keep rolling. It was the hunt not the quarry.

That wasn't the way it was for the old man. As we packed up the Leviathan he got more worked up than ever. He told me that Mechanicsburg was going to be home for us. He described it like he'd been there and come back to tell me about it. To him it was a place where men came together to build something better and turn back the curse that had reduced them to predators and prey. We'd be safe there. We'd be welcome there.

"Men with our skills. They'll have a place for us, you'll see," he said.

"Maybe they won't. Maybe they're full of more mouths than they can feed," I said.

"It's not that way, son. Not that way. They don't look at the world like there's only so much to go around. They don't accept the conditions as they're handed to them. They're like us, you and me, they work to make what they need. They've taken up God's challenge and mean to do more than just survive," he said, eyes gleaming wet.

That was his hope. That's what he held close to him, as close as that book of his. He thought we'd meet men that were like him, men who hadn't lost the way. The Word, as he put it. They'd be filled with promise and welcome more who believed as they did.

"Not belief in Jesus, son. Not in the inspired word of God, you understand. But they will believe in a future. They will believe in a better world than the sinful place we've inherited. And whether they know a God or not they will be in His grace because they stand ready to make good, to give and not just take," he said.

He'd lived longer than me so I assigned wisdom to him. Only there's one piece of wisdom I've gathered since I was a kid back in the warm hole.

It's not the number of days you've lived till this one.

It's the number of miles you've come to where you are.

As you roll across the trestle
Spanning Jordan's swelling tide
You will reach the Union Depot
Into which your train will ride

There you'll meet the superintendent
God the father, God the son
With a happy joyous greeting
Weary pilgrim, welcome home

Blessed Savior there to guide us
Till we reach that blissful shore
And the angels there to join us
In God's grace forevermore

The Boss sang as we rode up out of the longest tunnel and up to the surface. The sun was a disc of muted glare in a sky of rusted steel.

The treads crushed the last of a barricade of loose set concrete blocks that I'd torn down using the winch. Who knows how long ago the Boss and his crew had put that wall up to keep the curious out. Those nameless men, long dead, building a barricade to keep the world out. It was just blocks piled up with a big keystone set in the center. The keystone had an iron ring bolt crusted with rust set in it. I threaded a heavy chain through the bolt. I ran the winch mounted on the nose of the Leviathan to haul the anchor stone away. The whole thing collapsed in a dusty heap letting the sun into the tunnel for the first time since before I was even born.

We had some old paper maps with names and places that meant nothing to us, nothing to anyone anymore. The Boss thought he knew where we were on one of them. It all looked like stains and squiggles to me. There was a roadway that we'd find if we kept the Snake to our left. We go right on that road and follow it right to where the map was marked Mechanicsburg. Only I could see the name Mechanicsburg was written in by hand. I didn't ask by who.

Not that I cared. I was behind the wheel of the most badass machine in the world. It was like being drunk without drinking. The power of it made me giddy.

The cabin sat way up high on the legs. We could see miles ahead and around us as we trundled over the crusty ice along the flat banks of the Snake. The engine roared behind us. I could feel the power of it through my hands. Through my feet I could feel the bite of the big triangular treads clawing their way over the cold ground like the feet of a giant cat. We made a steady thirty per and the big shocks on the massive legs made the ride as smooth as if we were sailing on ice.

The cabin got so toasty I had to open a vent to let some cold air in. The old man sang his song and I looked in the rear view mirror and saw a big sloppy grin on my face.

That is one happy asshole, I thought.

It didn't matter where we were going. We were *going* and that's all that counted to me.

It was afternoon when we dropped down a long gentle slope to ride on the surface of the Snake itself. I knew there was a collection of ruins ahead and wanted to move around them. The old man suggested travelling further from the banks, away from the ice river to skirt the ruins. I told him we'd lose our direction doing that. If this road he was looking for crossed the Snake then following the course the ice took would take us there. There was no telling what kind of country we'd run across on higher ground.

From way up in my seat I could see figures coming out on the banks to watch us pass. We were moving too fast and too far out of range for them to shoot at us.

"Take a good look, fuckers," I shouted.

"No need to be unkind," the Boss said.

"You know they'd kill us and skin us and never have a single regret, Boss," I said.

"They're God's children, son. Just as we are," he said.

He said some more about forgiveness and redemption. All I could think was that some of God's children were sons of bitches lower than rat shit. I didn't say anything. I did wonder if, when our backs were against it, would the old man do anything more than pray.

Cilla's words were in my head like she was right there with me. She was telling me that having the old man along was worse than being alone. When we ran into bad shit it would be me carrying him. With his bent and crippled hands he couldn't work a gun or even drive the Leviathan. He could barely feed himself. I crushed her voice down in my head by thinking of how much I owed the Boss. He could have turned me away but he didn't. He gave me a life. He gave me a name. Cilla was only a whisper in my thoughts but her voice was still there.

I was too excited to sleep so I kept on through the night while the old man ratcheted his seat back and dozed off. There was a big rack of lights strung up over the cabin. I didn't flip them on. With the liquid light of the moon shining on the ice ahead I didn't need them. The Snake was a silvery path in the dark curving along between the black shoulders of hills either side.

Besides, as flat-out as we were moving, those lights would let anyone know we were coming from miles away. Plenty of time to set up a blockade or ambush. So I ran dark to reduce the chance of any ugly surprises in our way.

My eyes were getting heavy as I drove on into dawn. The weather was building to something nasty with the cloud cover dropping to the horizon. When it hit, it hit hard with sideways wind and thick snowfall backed by rolling thunder.

We weren't going to get better cover than that so I geared the engine to an idle. I braked us in the middle of the Snake. The old man woke up and I told him I'd be climbing into the back for a while. I left him sitting, looking out at the storm that rushed around us in a silent wave of white. I crawled into the womb of the sleep compartment and pulled the heavy curtain closed behind me. Within seconds I was into the deepest sleep I can remember, listening to the steady heartbeat of the Leviathan all around me.

The snow was falling light and piling heavy. It drifted down thick as a fog. The world was only what I could see just past the end of my fingers.

A woman was crying. The only sound in the quiet. I looked for her turning every way. All was swirling white. I moved to where I thought the sound was coming from.

The snow was stacked to my knees. I moved slow, every step an effort. My feet weighing more and more. My boots heavy with wet snow.

A gray shape shimmered, moving away from me. It was a woman. She held a blanket over her head like a hood. I tried to call out. I had no voice. I tried to run but the snow was heaped up to my thighs. I was wading with hands stretched out.

The woman's cry was a high continuous wail. Before she vanished into the blinding haze, she turned her head to look back. All I saw was the open maw of a mouth. Blood smeared teeth and that keening noise coming from deep within.

I hit my head sitting up in the sleeping compartment.

The cry was still there. It was the wind. The Leviathan shuddered under the gusts. I parted the curtain. Gray light came through the parts of the glass that weren't covered with ice crust. The Boss sat where I left him, seat fully reclined and sound asleep.

I lay back and rubbed the top of my head where I struck the hull. I wondered what the dream meant, if dreams meant anything. The woman. My mother. Cilla. The girl in the yellow parka. I didn't know if she was leading me somewhere or running away from me.

My head hurt and not just from smacking my skull on the ceiling. There was an iron taste in my mouth and I felt dizzy.

I pulled myself out, fighting down the urge to vomit. I worked the crank to open vents to let sweet cold air in. The old man was lying still with his mouth wide open. I slapped him hard on the face, hard enough to make my hand numb. It took me three times to get a response. He came around retching and gagging.

"Stay awake," I shouted to him.

"I feel sick," he said.

"I don't care. Stand up and breathe in the air from the vent," I said and lifted him out of the seat.

I pulled on my parka and got the driver side hatch open. It took putting my shoulder to it to break out of the ice coat.

The wind snatched it open with enough force to tug me out with it. My boots found the narrow running ramp and I hugged the cabin close to hang on. The wind tore at me, the keening moan turned to a scream in my ears. Near-blind, I used anything I could grip to pull myself to the engine housing. I climbed up on top using the recessed hand holds, slick with slushy snow melted in place by the warmth of the cowling.

The engine was chugging with an irregular pulse, struggling to breathe. I was on top of the Leviathan and crawling to the twin exhaust stacks. I designed them along with the Boss. We split the manifold into a duel system to prevent just what was happening now. It was my idea to put weather caps on them after what happened to those two wasters back in the Beast.

The lids on the caps were frozen wide open with clots of ice build-up acting like a stopper on them.

I gripped one of the hot exhaust pipes and used the hilt of my knife to hammer the ice free. The engine under me sucked in air with a shriek. A thick belch of diesel fumes blew out of the pipe. The wind whipped it away in ribbons of black. Steam rose from the vents, melting the crust over them. I did the same to the other pipe and the engine settled back into a regular rumble.

Climbing back to the cab I looked down to see the snow had drifted up over the treads burying them from view.

Inside the cab the old man was woozy but still standing. The trip through the blasting cold had cleared my head mostly. I told the Boss to stand by the open door and let the air into his lungs. I was aching and worn-out and wanted to do nothing more than lay down. I knew I couldn't do that. I had to keep us both alive.

Ice was riming the inside the of the cabin's windows. I pulled the Boss back away from the door and pulled it shut, the wind fighting me for every inch. I dogged it closed with what felt like the last of what I had. I heated some water on a plate we rigged up. I melted chocolate bars in it. The old man and I sat sipping it, holding our fingers over the top of our mugs to hold the heat in. We sat listening to the wind rise and fall.

"No point moving in this," he said after a while.

"Can't see for the white. We'd only get lost. Or run off a ledge," I agreed.

"There was a time you could tell which way you were going without being able to see," he said and tapped a gauge on the dash.

"I wondered what that did," I said.

"See that arrow. That always pointed north. You used that arrow and a map and you could never get lost. You could always know which direction you were heading," he said.

"Is it broken."

"Something is. The arrow doesn't line up with the map anymore. No true readings. The arrow's moving now, see it. It's not staying true."

"Maybe it's the wind," I said.

"No. Something else is acting on it. The arrow wants to point north but can't find it. It's like north isn't north these days. Like the whole world's broken and nothing works like it should," he said.

I said nothing.

"These are the end times, son. Just like the book tells us. The Lord hasn't abandoned us. He's challenging us. He'll deliver us in the end, the ones who adhered to his word and stayed on the narrow path. It might not be my lifetime or yours but he will be among us again," the old man said, but he wasn't talking to me anymore.

W e stayed in that place two more days till the storm blew itself out. I had to climb outside a couple more times to clear the exhausts of ice clogs.

When visibility returned and it came time to move again the treads wouldn't budge. They were stuck to the ice. We might gun that engine until the old man's Lord came back and not break out of that grip. I could use the winch but we were on a flat river plain. There was nothing to hook the chains to anywhere in sight.

It was another whole day of digging to clean the snow away to reveal the treads. They were locked down on the pack ice by a foot-thick layer of slush that froze into a pan as hard as steel. It would freeze over almost as fast as I could chip it away. The worst part was that we were sitting skylined where any nomad wasters could see us. As long as the storm covered us we were safe. Now we were bait for any asshole with a rifle and an empty belly.

I unlatched a can of the Boss's alcohol and poured it around the foot of each tread. Vapor rose off it to turn my stomach. It was an evil brew. I used a second can until I had a thin pool all around the base of the machine.

Something reached me on the wind as I poured the last splashes out of the second can. A faint sound through the gusts. I jerked my head up to see figures far off on the snow and getting closer. They spread out in a line. I could hear them calling to one another, or maybe me, only I couldn't make out any words.

The Boss wanted to know what I was up to when I climbed back into the cabin. He could smell the hooch rising up. I didn't answer him.

"We can stay here and find out what those guys want or we can get our asses out of here, Boss," I said.

I pulled the revolver to set by me on the console and pressed the clutch down. I slid the shifter into first. I kept my foot on the clutch while I used a striker to light a bit of greasy rag I had tied around an empty bottle for weight.

The figures were closer now. They were calling and waving hands. One held a rifle over his head. They were wasters. They'd kill us, rape us and eat us in one order or another.

I levered the door open enough to drop the flaming rag and bottle down into the pool of alkie.

It lit with a whoosh that sent a scorching wind up under the cabin. I let up on the clutch while feeding her some fuel. Leviathan lurched forward hard then rested back. I fed her more diesel and moved the shifter to second. She rocked forward again then back then forward again like a big bear on the rut.

A white star appeared in the windshield in front of me. The bullet buried itself in the cabin ceiling. Those men were running now, or trying to in the deep of the fresh fall. One of them stood and aimed his rifle again. I could see him through the shimmer of hot air rising from the lake of fire we sat in.

We could smell burning paint as the flames licked up the treads to the legs the cabin sat on. That fire was climbing toward the cans of the Boss' bad brew. We'd be roasted in our own machine if that happened, a damned hot meal for the assholes stalking us.

A second round came through the double-glazed windscreen and punched into my seatback.

I slammed her into third and prayed the big engine wouldn't stall on me. A sloshing and grinding noise came from below. The cabin shimmied and slewed rough to the right. I could feel the treads answering through my hands. She was breaking loose. I had to be ready when the treads came free or flip her on her side.

We broke out with a heave and I fought the wheel to put her straight. We rolled out of the fire, leaving a burning trail behind us. The fire had melted some of the ice on the Leviathan. The melt made an opaque layer of frost over all the cabin's glass. I was blind so I kept her straight the only way I knew how—by keeping the CAT symbol upright at the center of the wheel. I revved her up to overdrive.

I guess I ran straight into the line of dumbass wasters. Even over the engine roar I could hear a high scream cut short as we trundled over a bump in the snow.

We heard a few metallic rings off the back plates as they fired a few farewell shots in frustration. I kept rolling on till I was satisfied we were well clear of those guys. I climbed out cautiously and checked us over for any damage from the bullets or the fire.

I found a mess of greasy paste infused with hair stuck between the bogey wheels and the treads. One of those guys was slow to get out of the way. There were a couple of discs of missing paint where bullets struck the engine housing without doing any real damage. The fuel tank was still intact and not holed anywhere.

The treads were scorched black and the paint melted off the legs above them. The underside of the raised cab was bubbled by the heat but was still solid. We were still on wide-open ground with nothing and no one in sight. I took the time to oil the treads and wheel assemblies. The fire for sure scorched them dry.

I climbed back to the cab to stand on the ramp and survey the country around us. Way off to our left I could make out the silvery line of the Snake curving away. Off ahead of us the black skeleton of a bridge crossed the river of ice.

We got going again and didn't see anyone else on the horizon the rest of the day.

The next day we found the highway and the path that led to Mechanicsburg.

T he skies were clear in the days that followed the storm. The
winds were still and a hard chill bore down in the still air. The
white disc of the sun shone in a hard and empty sky. At night the
moon rose large against a field of stars.

We ran at night with the lights out and I could lean back and look
up through the double-glazed port on top of the cab and make myself
dizzy looking into the endless black.

We found the highway the same day we broke out of the ice. It came
off the end of a black suspension bridge where a crooked sign hung
from the cross supports. The Boss said the number on the sign matched
the number on his old map.

I slung a right and put us on a mostly flat surface moving straight as
string away from the Snake. It was a good thing that the cabin was
perched up so high. From there we could see the road was clearly
drawn, an uninterrupted band with the surface kept level by the wind.
In places it was marked by the drifted humps of buildings on either
side, or by crooked poles trailing tangles of wires to the snow.

It passed through small settlements and people either ran from us
or came out to watch us pass in silence. The further we left the Snake
behind us the more folks ran when they saw us coming.

"A godless land," the Boss said more times than I can remember.

The days of driving were tiring. I had to be in the seat from dark to
dark, sometimes only pausing long enough to take a piss. The old man
slept most of the time leaving me alone at the wheel. Sometimes in the
long hours I'd find myself humming that song about crossing Jordan

on a railway. It's the only song I knew. Hell, it was the only music I'd ever heard in my life. The words meant nothing to me but the tune stuck in my mind and found its way out once in a while.

Driving was no longer a childish thrill. After hours and days at the wheel it changed into work. Then it turned to second nature, leaving my mind free to wander.

I thought of Cilla then. I thought about how she could be here with us sharing the adventure of it all. Then I'd remember why she wasn't here. Some more road would pass under the cab and I'd start thinking about her again, starting at the beginning, wishing she was with us.

I could only sleep when we were sure we were far from any human eyes. I'd wait until full dark and find a place where the Leviathan wouldn't stand alone against the sky. Once I pulled up to the base of a tall steel tower. It was one in a row of towers that could be seen marching off in either direction all the way to the horizon.

Another time I pulled under a high bridge, a road passing overheard. I got up the next morning to dump the shit bucket and saw boot prints in the snow around the treads. That shook me. They moved on without bothering us. Or maybe they went to get more of their friends. I didn't say anything to the old man. I just pulled away and put the place far behind us.

Lots of times we saw animals. Wolves chased us once for a mile or so, baying and snapping. Once we saw a line of barrel-chested animals moving along the edge of some pines. The Boss told me they were pigs, wild boar. He said they were good eating but mean.

A few times we saw big herds of caribou, dotted over the white land for miles. I wanted to stop the machine and take one down, tie it down on top of the Leviathan and let it freeze solid for later. The old man told me to keep driving.

"We're getting close," he said.

"Mechanicsburg."

I don't know how he could know that. When he was awake he either read his book or studied that map, holding it close to his old eyes like he'd see something there he missed before. Mechanicsburg was ahead. He told me he knew it. He told me that God would not have led him this far to abandon him. All of the years and toil and pain would not be time spent in vain. That's what he said and that's what he believed so I dropped us into higher gear and motored on.

We were going through fuel faster than the Boss figured on. We'd come close to five hundred miles according to the odometer on the dash. The old man marked our path along the highway on the map using landmarks that he'd match to place names. The tank was sloshing away behind us. I didn't have enough in the cans to top it off. We started looking for fuel.

There were places where the highway met another wide strip going over a crossroads. Here we found buildings with names like 66 and Shell. They were collapsed under the burden of tons of pack ice. I looked for depressions where others had dug the frozen cover away. The openings to the gas tanks were there. Most I found empty after digging them out. I found one with dregs in it after three tries. I ran a hose down and pumped cans full of gasoline and humped them two at a time to the Leviathan. The cans would have to be filtered. The gas was loaded with sediment.

It was tiring work. The worrying part was the most exhausting. The old man kept watch and would pull the lever for the horn if he saw anything. I tied the pull line around his wrist. I was never sure how much I could trust his eyes. It weighed on me as I pumped and carried.

I climbed up to secure the cans in place and I saw something move on the bridge over the highway. A head ducked down below a curtain wall. I kept watching and saw clouds of vapor rising from behind the wall. More than one person watched me while I pumped the fuel. They were hiding, waiting now. Letting me do all the work for them.

I left two cans behind and squeezed into the cabin. I got the Leviathan moving and swung her around to go around the bridge instead of under it. Ambush spoiled. I brought the truck onto the highway on the other side of the span. Looking back, I saw men climbing on machines on top of the bridge. In the rearview I saw them start the machines in thick clouds of exhaust. They came down the ramps and started after us in a pack.

Even with me running flat out and all gauges redlined, they caught up to us in a hurry. There were three of them on motorbikes like the one Fingers had back in the Beast. Spiked tires with seats set high. The riders wore tooled leather outfits and helmets with dark visors that hid their faces. They had rifles in boots mounted to the frames but didn't touch them. They looked up at me as they slowed alongside. I drove with one hand on the wheel and the other holding my revolver trained on them through the glass, letting them see it.

They sped up and passed us to tear along down the highway and out of sight over the crest of a rise.

"Mechanicsburg! They're from Mechanicsburg for sure," the Boss whooped.

"How can you know that," I said.

"They didn't shoot at us. They let you be while you fueled up. They're probably riding ahead to tell their friends we're on our way to Mechanicsburg," he said and beamed at me with wet eyes.

They didn't attack when they could of. The old man was right about that. But he was wrong about why they didn't. This was the big empty world we were in. They watched us to make sure we were real, to see if we were a threat and how much of a threat we might be. They wanted to decide if me and the Boss were someone to stay away from or someone to stalk.

It was their highway, we were just driving on it. And they had the big edge on us. They knew where we were going and we didn't.

A hundred more miles on down the highway we saw a white cloud rising from the ground somewhere close to the horizon. It spread up into the clear blue sky where high winds caught it and pulled it to wispy shreds.

The sun dropped behind us throwing our shadow far ahead, pointing like a finger straight to the growing cloud. The last rays lit the column white against the darkening blue. The highway ran right toward it like the line on the map where the old man marked Mechanicsburg. Whatever was at the end of our road, it made that giant cloud.

"It's industry, son. It's men working with other men to make something better," the Boss said.

"You so sure about that," I said.

"That's exhaust of some kind. It's not smoke, it's not from a fire. It's stationary so it means they have controlled, man-made heat. It's Mechanicsburg, it has to be," he said.

I shrugged.

"You have to have faith, son. You have to believe in things you can't see, things outside of yourself," he said.

"It's man-made, you say. That means men. I can't have faith in men I don't know. The ones I have known turned out not to be worth shit," I said.

"And me. Is that how you see me," the old man said.

"Not you, Boss. You're like that Jesus guy you read to me about. Too good to be true. I have faith in you," I said.

"And Jesus," he said.

"I'll judge him when I meet him," I said.

"When you meet him it's too late," he said.

"It's too late anyway," I said.

He didn't say more after that. The Boss just sat holding his book to him with his gnarled hands.

The rising cloud was blanking out the stars ahead of us. A rim of light grew higher and wider at its base.

Steep hills dropped down either side of the highway. The slopes were hedged with dense pines clinging on below the wind line. It felt to me like hands closing on us as the light bloomed brighter ahead.

I flipped on our own lamp array to show us the road ahead. We weren't hiding from anyone anymore. They knew we were coming. I saw the bike tracks crisscrossing ahead of us the whole day. Those guys were scouts. They'd been to wherever they were headed hours ahead of us. Their tracks showed clear in the wide pool of light we projected before us.

A dark bar took shape ahead of the Leviathan. It grew to a black barrier across the roadway from slope to sheltering slope. When I was close enough to see figures back-lighted atop it, I geared down and braked the machine.

The old man was breathing shallow and staring ahead. I sat listening to the engine ticking over, its power coming through my feet and hands like an animal eager to break from a leash. Maybe it was telling me to turn around and run like hell. Something was telling me that, screaming the words inside my head.

"We are here. God has brought us home," the Boss said. His voice caught in a wet choke. Tears were rolling down his face.

"You sure. This what you want to do. Throw it all in with these guys. We can turn around. Last chance," I said.

"Faith, son. Have faith," he said.

I touched the smooth butt of my revolver, making sure it was snug under my belt.

A light source started as a sliver at the center of the bar of black. It grew wider like an opening eye. A bright beam reached out for us. Hazy figures moved on the ice in the glare of it.

"We're being welcomed," the Boss said.

I put her in gear and we rolled ahead slow.

As we got closer I could see that the blockade ahead was made up of trucks with slabs of steel plate mounted on one side to make a moveable wall across the highway. I drove through the gap made when they pulled a truck aside. Men stood on the tops of the trucks and were level with the cab of the Leviathan as we rolled past. They all had rifles or shotguns. No one aimed at us. One of them waved us along. I could tell by all the vapor coming through the holes in his mask that he was shouting to us. I couldn't hear the words through the double-glaze and our engine sounds. It was plain enough what he wanted. I kept up our slow pace through the gate.

There were berms of snow piled up on either side of the opening. That left me hemmed in with one path to drive. With the four legs independently suspended we could have climbed over the berms. Only there was no room to turn the Leviathan. I'd tip us over trying.

Men on top of the berm kept up with us at a trot. The berms fell away after fifty feet or so. We were back out on the broad highway surface with lights strung up all around. I was blinded. I couldn't see past the lights to what was further along the roadway. Motorbikes came out of the brightness and slew to a stop in front of us. Five riders. I recognized a couple of them as the guys we saw back at the Shell. They sat straddling their bikes holding rifles in their hands.

One of them dismounted and made a quick cutting motion with his hand. I geared down to idle. I shut down the lights. He walked closer until he was below the Leviathan on my side.

I cracked the door open and stepped out onto the running ramp. The revolver felt heavy against my belly. The man took off his helmet to look up at me. He had a hard face lined by the sun. His head was covered in a close-fitting hood of black cloth. Gray eyebrows sprouted against the dark cloth. There was a handgun in a flap holster on the belt around his leather cover-all. The flap was latched down. His hands didn't stray near it.

"How many are you," the man called up to me. His voice held nothing in it that told me anything. That told me everything.

"Two. Me and an old man," I said.

"Where you going to. You have a home somewhere. People. Or are you wasters."

"Here. We're coming here."

"Yah. And where's here," he said tilting his head.

"Mechanicsburg," I said trying not to make it sound like a question.

"Then you're here," he said.

"This is Mechanicsburg," I said looking into his eyes, trying to see the truth in them.

"It is. Climb down out of there. Bring the old man," he said and stepped back.

I helped the Boss out of his seat and onto the ramp. I climbed down the ladder ahead of him, guiding him slowly to the ice a rung at a time. More people had come as we came down. They stood at the edges of the light. I saw women and children and more men with more guns. They watched us without talking to one another. Each of them finding their own answers as they watched me helping the old man over the ice to where the black-hooded man stood. Without a word from him some of the bike riders trotted forward to join him.

The Boss dropped to his knees before them. Somehow he managed to keep that book held against his body the whole way down the ladder. I felt a rifle butt tap me between the shoulders then behind one knee.

I went down on the ice on all fours beside the old man.

"I have prayed with conviction. I have prayed with faith. The Lord has provided and shown us the way," he said raising a quavering hand, fingers bent and knuckles swollen red.

"God brought you here," the black hood said.

"He has delivered us into your hands. Blessed God has taken us from the wilderness to join you," the old man said, his tears freezing on his face in silver cords.

The man in the black hood drew the gun from his holster. He put two rounds into the old man's head one behind the other. The old man leaned back on his heels, head bobbing twice. He stayed like that, on his knees, arms at his side. The book lay on the ice with the wind riffling the pages.

I felt the hot barrel press down on the top of my head. I kept my eyes lowered, watching the shadow of the man on the ice.

"How about you, boy. God bring you here too," the man said.

"I don't have any god," I said.

"Then what brought you to Mechanicsburg, boy," the man said.

"The machine. I built it. I worked my ass off to build it and now you assholes are going to take it away," I said. No bitterness. Statement of fact.

The man made a noise between his teeth. The pressure of the hot gun barrel came off my head. Hands pulled me to my feet. More hands tore open my outer clothes and found the revolver and bone-handled knife. I stood blinking into the light giving them nothing.

No fear. No hate. They were going to do what they were going to do. The only choice I had left was not to go out like a whining bitch.

A hand shoved me forward to follow the man in the black hood through the corona of lights and into the surrounding crowd. They parted in front of him. Hands gripped my arms to guide me forward. We walked off the smooth surface of the highway onto a down-sloping pathway through trees into a collection of low buildings that were nothing but hummocks of snow with lit doorways dug away for entry.

I followed, or was shoved, behind the black hood down a block-walled corridor into a place with a high ceiling. More corridors fed off this room in either direction. I was guided along one. The walls were lined either side with roll-up doors that had numbers painted on them and heavy locks hanging from hasps. We stopped at one marked 1-1058. Black hood undid a lock and yanked a pull rope up to draw the door open with a rattling sound.

I was shoved inside. The only look I got as the door was drawn down behind was a room with three block walls, a bare concrete floor and a ceiling covered over with wire mesh.

Once the door was closed it was total black. After a time I could see a faint glow of light coming down through the wire mesh ceiling from somewhere else in the building.

I sat down in a corner of the room away from the door and huddled tight to hold in as much heat as I had left.

They might have had a way of watching me so I put my face in my hands until I fell asleep.

This was the end of the road. My mind and body came apart then. For the better or the worst it was over. All I knew was release. I let it go and gave in.

T here was more light coming down through the mesh when the door opened. The sun had come up while I was out.

The man in the black hood the night before stepped inside. His hood was down showing a brush of white hair. He was in dark clothes. The gunbelt was still around his waist. He was alone. I guess I wasn't much of a threat.

"You really build that machine out there," he said.

"Not all of it. I finished the motor. Got her running," I said.

"How far you come," he said.

"Six or seven hundred miles off the Snake."

"The river."

"Yah. We had a garage there. Just us two. Me and the Boss," I said.

"He kin to you. He your dad," he said.

"Just a guy."

"Were you lying last night. The old man talking all that God shit. You rode with him. You weren't of a mind to see things his way."

"He talked God all the time. I never listened," I said.

"All right," he said.

"You don't believe in God in Mechanicsburg," I said.

"We believe in Him. We hate Him," the man said and brought the door down to leave me alone.

T hey brought me food later that day. The man and a woman
about his same age. She didn't say anything while he stood in
the door watching. She set down a tray with a bowl of hot food and
a plate of bread and a jar of clean water. She stepped back into the
hallway and came back with a steel bucket she set in a corner of the
room. Then she left us alone.

The bowl was a thick stew of caribou with chunks of vegetables. It
was salty and rich and I dug into it like digging a trench. The bread
was the first I'd ever seen. It was crusty and chewy.

"If you're as good with your hands as you said you might earn yourself a place here. Not up to me. We have a council here and they'll decide," the man said.

He didn't tell me his name and didn't ask mine. That let me know
what it was they were deciding. Why learn a name you'd never use.
One they'd forget soon enough.

"You have machines, I can fix them and keep them running right,"
I said. Not begging just telling him.

"We'll test you on that depending on what the council comes up
with," he said.

"I'll show you. I'll earn my place."

"Not like that old man. He was done, boy. You know that. Another
empty belly, is all," he said. Not making excuses, just telling me.

I looked up from the bowl to meet his eyes. I looked for something
there and didn't find it. He was looking for something in me but I gave
nothing in return. I went back to wiping the bowl with the bread to get

WINTERWORLD ❄ CHUCK DIXON

the last of the gravy. He brought the door down with a bang and left me in the gloom.

Want to judge me. Go ahead. Bring your council and take a vote. Bring down God and the savior themselves. Send me across Jordan or to perdition. None of it could be worse than going on living in a world where every asshole you ran into thought he had a right to decide if you were either worth feeding or feeding to the dogs.

I didn't kill the Boss. He was dead the first time he heard of this place only all it took was getting him here to meet that bullet. There was no place for him here. It wasn't the place he thought it was. Mechanicsburg was a place where men worked with men to make their lives better. Their own lives. Only they wanted no part of the old man's God or his book and mostly they wanted no part of him.

I was young and strong and had a skill they might need. When it came time to test me I was going to prove to them that I'd earn my place here. Maybe they'd decide the other way and I'd get a bullet in the skull. That was up to them.

Right then, for that minute or the next hour, I had a full belly and a warm place to sleep.

And that was enough.

LOST IN TIME…
DAMNED BY FATE?

"Chuck is a damn good writer who is really good at hooking you, giving you fun characters, and telling you one hell of an adventure story."
— Larry Correia, Monster Hunters International, the Grimoir Chronicles

CHUCK DIXON'S action-packed, thrill-driven new series of novels featuring time-travelling Army Rangers facing the past's most dangerous threats and deadliest armies.

www.dixonverse.net